W9-BGO-759

BOOST

BOOST

STEVE BREWER

speck press
denver

Printed and bound in Canada.
Book layout and design by *Magpie*, magpiecreativedesign.com

This book is a work of fiction. Names, characters, places and incidents
are either the product of the author's imagination or are used fictitiously.
Any resemblance to actual events or locales or persons, living or dead,
is entirely coincidental. Although the author and publisher have made
every effort to ensure the accuracy and completeness of information
contained in this book, we assume no responsibility for errors,
inaccuracies, omissions, or any inconsistency herein. Any slights of
people, places or organizations are unintentional.

Library of Congress Cataloging-in-Publication Data

Brewer, Steve.
Boost / by Steve Brewer.
p. cm.
ISBN 0-9725776-5-3
1. Albuquerque (N.M.)--Fiction. 2. Informers--Crimes against--
Fiction. 3. Automobile theft--Fiction. I. Title.

PS3552.R42135B66 2004
813'.54--dc22

2004016222

10 9 8 7 6 5 4 3 2 1

As always, for Kelly.

1

THE PROBLEM WITH boosting classic cars is they're so damned conspicuous. Steal a brand-new pickup truck or a run-of-the-mill Toyota and you can drive it for days before some cop might get lucky and nab you. But tool around a car-crazy town like Albuquerque in a hot 1965 Thunderbird with a gold metal-flake paint job and people notice. And that's just asking for trouble.

Sam Hill knew he should take the stolen T-Bird directly to Mitch's Auto Salvage and collect his four grand. But he was thirsty, and what could it hurt to stop for a minute at a 7-Eleven, pick up a Big Gulp?

The Thunderbird drove smoothly, its eight-cylinder engine throbbing under the long hood. The wide-bodied car was heavy as a tank—old-fashioned Detroit steel—but it rode like a boat on calm waters, barely registering the potholes and patches that made the ramshackle commercial strip of North Fourth Street a hazardous obstacle course. Sam guessed the owner, a lawyer named Timothy Blankenship, had completely replaced the suspension system. Sam spun the steering wheel with one gloved hand and the car floated up into the brightly lit convenience store parking lot.

He nosed the car into a slot by the door, cut the engine, and climbed out. His reflection in the store's tall windows showed that he and the T-Bird made a pretty good match. He was dressed all in black, as usual, which complemented the car's black vinyl roof, and the gold paint set off his honey-blond hair. Sam's cheekbones jutted like the car's fenders, and his too-wide mouth mimicked the T-Bird's grille. A lean build, though he looked bulkier thanks to his black leather jacket, which was a heavy biker model made all the heavier by the stuff stashed in its pockets—a ten-inch screwdriver, a ring of forty keys, a cell phone, a Mini-Mag flashlight, and a set of lock picks in a suede pouch. Tools of the trade, weighing him down.

He hadn't needed most of the gear to steal the T-Bird—a copy of the car's key had been provided by the client who commissioned the theft. Blankenship kept his prized auto in an old wooden garage behind his rambling North Valley house, a padlock on the door. Sam's screwdriver made quick work of the hasp, then he'd used it to pop the metal cover off the alarm system. He'd yanked the wires loose by the third "whoop." No one had come around, wondering about the noise. Alarms go off all the time. People consider them a nuisance, if they register the sound at all. Besides, it was early-winter dusk, the flaming New Mexico sunset fading in the west, and most neighbors hadn't even been home from work.

Sam stepped up onto the sidewalk in front of the store, his breath fogging in the chill November air. A police car pulled into the lot, parked right next to the hot T-Bird.

Oh, shit. Sam hesitated. Should he go into the 7-Eleven, act like everything's fine? Had the cop seen him getting out of the car? If so, Sam couldn't just walk away without raising suspicions.

The cop got out of his Crown Vic patrol car and joined Sam on the sidewalk. He was a couple of inches taller than Sam's six feet, and bulging muscles stretched the shoulder seams of his dark uniform. Looked to be in his late twenties, maybe ten years younger than Sam. The cop flashed perfect white teeth.

"Nice car," he said. "What year?"

"It's a '65."

The cop stopped in front of the T-Bird's long hood. "Restore it yourself?"

"Nah, I don't know anything about cars. Paid a small fortune to have it done."

"They did a great job."

"Thanks." Sam needed to end this conversation, get his Big Gulp, and get the hell out of there. Just his luck, the cop had to be a car nut.

A muted chirp started up, sounded like it was coming from the T-Bird. Sam had checked the car for an alarm, had found none. Had he overlooked something?

The cop pulled a cell phone off his utility belt and checked the readout. "Not mine," he said. "You got a phone in the car?"

Sam knew very well that his cell phone was in his jacket, but he patted his pockets like he was looking for one. The cop was right. That was a phone ringing.

"Sounds like it's coming from the trunk."

"Oh, yeah," Sam said. "I must've left it in my gym bag."

Gym bag. Where the heck had that come from? Sam hadn't been inside a gym since high school.

The chirping stopped after the fifth ring. The cop showed his bright smile again. "Too late."

"Probably not important. They'll call back."

They headed into the 7-Eleven, Sam hoping the relief hadn't shown on his face. Before they could get through the door, the ringing started again.

Shit, shit, shit. Sam shrugged. "Guess I'd better answer it."

He pulled the T-Bird's key from the pocket of his black jeans as he hurried to the rear of the golden car. Glanced back, saw the cop standing in the store doorway, watching. Two clerks in red tunics were behind the counter, eyeballing them. Sam hoped the key worked in the trunk. If it didn't, it would set them to wondering.

The flat trunk lid popped open. Sam lifted it, and his stomach flopped when he saw what was inside. A man was in there, curled up in a fetal position. A very dead man.

The corpse was skinny, wearing faded jeans, and a blue shirt. His face was turned up toward the sky and he had a bullet hole between his heavy black eyebrows. The blood-encrusted hole pushed his brown eyes apart, making them bulge outward, like the guy was trying to peer into his own ears.

Sam caught himself before he yelped in surprise. Trying to keep the shock off his face, he glanced at the patrolman, who still stood watching. The raised lid blocked his view of the inside of the trunk, but Sam needed to close it in a hurry.

The phone chirped again and he spotted it, face up on the trunk liner next to the dead guy. He snatched up the phone, hit its answer button, and held it up for the cop to see. Sam slammed the trunk, then put the phone to his ear and said, "Hello?" What else could he do?

"Tony?" said a man's voice. "That you?"

Sam kept his eyes on the cop, who gave him one last grin and went into the store. He thumbed off the phone, but kept it to his ear, nodding and moving his lips, as he went to the driver's side of the T-Bird. He couldn't see the cop inside the store, but that didn't mean he wasn't still watching from behind a rack of doughnuts. Sam made a show of looking at his wristwatch, then got behind the wheel and cranked the engine.

He backed the T-Bird away, keeping its rear license plate out of view from the store windows as long as possible. Then he whipped the car into the Fourth Street traffic and sped away.

2

SAM WIPED HIS forehead with a gloved hand as he steered the Thunderbird into the parking lot of U-Stor-It-Now. Sweat kept dripping into his eyes from his mop of blond hair, and it wasn't hot inside the car. Nerves.

He took a deep breath, blew it out loudly. Calm down, boy. Nobody knows there's a corpse in the trunk. You've made it to the storage unit. You're safe. For now.

He stopped the car outside unit twenty-three, headlights shining on the mustard-colored overhead door. U-Stor-It-Now consisted of three blocks of garage-style storage units arranged around a narrow parking lot. Plain gray concrete-block bunkers gouged with one ugly yellow door after another. An equally charming office fronted the lot at San Mateo Boulevard, but the windows were empty. Sam had met the manager, a grizzled old drunk who kept a portable TV going on the counter. This time of evening, you could drive a bulldozer into the lot and the bleary manager wouldn't even stagger over to the window to check out the noise.

The manager's lack of curiosity was one reason Sam kept the unit rented here, registered to "Justin Case," phony address, fake phone number. No way to trace it to Sam, and no one cared who really used it, as long as the monthly twenty-dollar rent was paid on time. He kept several units rented in different locations around the city, always paying in cash. Just in case.

The night air chilled the sweat on his face as he got out of the T-Bird. He left the engine running, pulled the key ring from his pocket, and stood in the headlight beams as he sorted through his many keys. He found the one for the Yale padlock that kept the garage secured, bent over to unlock it, then rolled the door up.

The headlights shone into the unit, illuminating a few cardboard boxes stacked in the far corners. The boxes were full of household items—dishes, books, records—junk Sam bought at yard sales and stored here so it would look right if anyone ever searched the place. Still plenty of room for a stolen car.

He drove the T-Bird into the storage unit, then got out and looked around the parking lot before closing the garage door. No light inside the storage unit; no electricity at all. The sudden darkness—and the knowledge of what was in the trunk—made him feel claustrophobic.

He flicked on his flashlight and squeezed between the roll-up door and the trunk of the T-Bird. Unlocked the trunk and lifted the lid. A light came on inside.

The corpse was just how he left it, looking deflated and bony. Sam felt a wave of nausea roll through him, and he huffed the stale air to steady himself. Poor bastard shot right between the eyes. Looked like a large-bore bullet. The back of the corpse's head was against the trunk liner, but Sam guessed a good portion of the skull was missing. Blood stiffened the man's oily black hair.

Sam's throat closed and he coughed against another jolt of nausea. He wanted to close the trunk, lock the car up in the storage unit, and walk away. But he couldn't just leave it here. Not for long. The smell of decay would alert someone eventually, and questions would follow. And cops.

He leaned into the trunk and went through the dead man's pockets. Wallet, comb, pocketknife, keys. Sam left everything but the wallet, which he took with him as he sidled around the car.

He used his flashlight to examine the wallet's contents. Two twenties, a Mobil credit card, a driver's license in the name of Antonio Armas, age twenty-eight, an address in Albuquerque's South Valley. No doubt this was "Tony," the guy who'd gotten the call on the cell phone.

"Tony can't come to the phone right now," Sam muttered as he put everything back in the billfold.

He squeezed through to the trunk, put the wallet back in the hip pocket of the dead man's jeans. Armas' shirt cuffs were unbuttoned and Sam pushed up the sleeves, found old track marks on the inside of his skinny arms. The veins were knotty and bulging, but he didn't find any fresh needle marks. Maybe Tony Armas was a reformed junkie. Or maybe he'd run out of good veins in his arms, had switched to his legs or between his toes.

The blue shirt was also unbuttoned in front, halfway down Armas' chest. Sam grasped one edge of the shirt, pulled it open. Something shiny caught the light and he pulled the shirt open further. A tiny microphone was attached to Armas' pale chest with flesh-colored tape. A wire ran from the microphone to his waist, then disappeared behind his back.

Sam's breath caught in his throat. Tony was wired for sound. But he couldn't be a cop, not with those track marks on his arms. Which meant he was an informant, trying to get close to somebody, probably a drug dealer.

"Shit," Sam said aloud. He slammed the trunk, then used the flashlight to make his way back around to the driver's side of the T-Bird.

What the hell was a wired-up dead man doing in the trunk of this car? Was the owner, Blankenship, some kind of dealer? That didn't fit. Blankenship was a lawyer. And the timing was too coincidental. Someone wanted Sam to steal the car while the corpse was in there. Make disposal of the body Sam's problem. Maybe even dropped a dime to the cops, telling them to watch for a fancy gold Thunderbird if they wanted to find their dead informant.

Smelled like a set-up, through and through. But who the hell would set Sam up? He had no enemies, at least none who'd go to this much trouble to nail him. Somebody had a problem with Sam, they'd come see him, right? Give him a roughing up or try to make him dead. That's the way of the Wild West. Face to face, man to man. This situation was like a very bad version of the practical jokes Sam loved to pull on others. A client sending him out to steal a particular car, providing the keys in advance, aware the corpse was in there.

Sam didn't know who'd requested the car. The order had come through Robin Mitchell, as usual. Sam and Robin had the same set-up he'd used with her father for years—somebody ordered a special car, Mitch tracked one down through Motor Vehicle Department records, gave Sam the address and other particulars. Sam delivered the car and took his cut of the money. Mitch (and since Mitch's death a year earlier from a heart attack, Robin) dealt with the clients, making the delivery and collecting the money. Sam had always wanted it this way. Less exposure for him.

Boosting collectible cars was more profitable than picking up random wheels around town. The buyer was already in place. The amount of time Sam was in possession of the hot car was minimal. And it was a hell of a lot more challenging. Somebody goes to a lot of trouble to lovingly restore some old car, they tend to keep it secure. Alarms, locks, the works. And most car nuts don't drive their prizes that often, so the chances of finding the car parked somewhere, easy to steal, were slim. The challenge kept it interesting for Sam, though the thought always tickled his mind that somebody might use him to get at a rival in the competitive world of cruisers and car shows.

But he'd never considered the idea that someone might use the arrangement to get to *him*. Auto theft had its risks, but they didn't include a wired corpse stashed in a trunk.

One thing was certain: Sam couldn't move the T-Bird. The car was too noticeable to drive around town while he sorted out what to do about the late Antonio Armas.

He fished his cell phone out of his pocket and hit the speed-dial. It rang three times as Sam whispered tightly, "Come on, come on."

"Hello?"

"Billy?"

"Hey, Sam. What's going on? I was just sitting around, watching a video. You ever see that war movie, 'The Thin Red Line?' Got Nick Nolte and Sean Penn—"

"Billy? Not now. I've got a problem."

Billy Suggs' voice came back hushed. "What's up?"

"I need a ride. I'm at that storage place on San Mateo. You remember which one I mean?"

"Sure."

"Pull up in front of my unit. I'm inside. I'll be listening for you."

"I'm on my way."

Sam stowed the phone in his pocket. He wasn't crazy about hiding in the storage unit while Billy drove halfway across town, but he didn't want to wait outside either.

He crept to the overhead door and stood listening. Nothing but silence outside.

A phone chirped. In the car. Sam got the door open and leaned inside to snatch Armas' phone off the passenger seat.

"Hello?"

"Tony?"

Sam hesitated. How could he hope to sound like Tony, when he'd never heard the dead man speak? Monosyllables.

"Yeah. Who's this?"

"You know who this is." The phone sounded crackly, its battery nearly dead. "You haven't been answering your phone. Where are you?"

Sam said nothing, his mind whirring. Was the man on the other end of the line a cop? A narc? A dealer?

"Tony?"

"Yeah?"

A long pause. Shit, Sam thought, he's onto me. Guess I don't sound like Tony.

"Who the hell is this?"

Sam punched a button to turn off the phone. He stuffed it in a jacket pocket, thinking he might need it later. No way for the cops to trace it as long as he left it off. Then he went back to listening by the door.

"Hurry, Billy," he whispered. "I need to get out of here."

3

BILLY SUGGS DOWNSHIFTED his Mustang as a traffic signal changed to yellow up ahead. Sam sounded like he had an emergency on his hands, but Billy knew the rules: Obey the traffic laws, don't attract attention. He wouldn't reach Sam any faster if some cop pulled him over for blowing through a red light.

Billy drummed on the steering wheel with his bony fingers while waiting for the green, beating out the rhythm of a song from the war movie's soundtrack. He caught himself doing it and forced his hands to stop. Billy was a high-strung guy, always in motion. Knees bouncing or hands drumming or toes tapping, playing along to the music in his head. Sam had tried to teach him to sit still. Keep your muscles relaxed, he'd said, so they're rested if you need to move in a hurry.

Sam regularly spouted such fatherly advice, some of which didn't make much sense to Billy. Wouldn't your muscles be more ready if they were already tensed? But he listened to Sam, tried to do whatever the older man told him. Sam had survived by his wits for two decades, living off stolen cars. If Billy wanted to follow his example—and he wanted nothing more—he'd take Sam's advice.

Take the Mustang, for example. When he first started working with Sam, he'd kept the navy-blue car buffed to a glossy shine. The car had fat tires and chrome rims and an exhaust system so loud it could blow windows out of nearby buildings. Sam ordered him to change all that. A stock muffler. Basic rims. No vanity plates or after-market crap like spoilers or fender skirts or painted flames, stuff you saw on cars all over Albuquerque.

"That's like putting a sign on your car," Sam had said.

"What kind of sign?"

"One that says, 'Hey, Mr. Policeman, please pull me over.' You want to beef up a car, do it under the hood. But leave the outside alone. Look like a citizen."

Good advice, Billy knew. And he'd taken it, even if it meant driving around in plain vanilla all the time, which was tough for a guy freshly twenty-one years old, a guy who loved cars and who absolutely *knew* a hot ride was a babe magnet. Most of the work Billy did for Sam consisted of driving—taking Sam someplace to boost a car, picking him up after he'd made a delivery. Sam wanted inconspicuous, that's what he'd get.

The light changed and the Mustang surged forward. Not much farther now. He'd memorized the locations of Sam's haunts months ago after Sam drove him around Albuquerque, showing him the places he used in his work and giving him copies of the keys. Sam shared such information with no one else. His trust made Billy feel privileged.

Signing on as Sam's apprentice was, to Billy's way of thinking, the best event in an otherwise shitty life. An orphan, Billy had floated from one crappy foster home to another his whole life, and he never had any kind of father figure until he met Sam two years earlier.

Billy had been broke then, a dropout, no job, no future at all. The only thing he knew, the only thing he really loved, was cars. He'd started boosting them, no idea what he was doing, just trying to make a buck, when he made the big mistake that led him to Sam.

Billy tried to steal a car off the lot behind Mitch's Auto Salvage. Middle of the night, no security guard, no snarling dogs, he'd taken his time, trying to get the starter of a primo '69 Camaro to turn over, when this big old bastard appeared beside the window, a cigar clenched tightly in his teeth and a shotgun in his hands.

Buford "Mitch" Mitchell, though Billy hadn't known it at the time. All he knew was this red-faced man was ready to splatter his brains all over the dashboard. Mitch ordered Billy out of the car and marched him into the garage, where a guy with blond hair and black clothes was waiting beside a desk covered with playing cards.

The two men discussed Billy's predicament like he hadn't been right there, hearing the whole thing. Mitch was ready to shoot Billy where he stood. But the other guy—Sam, of course—smiled and said it took balls to sneak into Mitch's lot to try to boost a ride, when everyone in Albuquerque (except Billy!) knew Mitch was more foul-tempered than a badger.

At Sam's suggestion, they ordered Billy back out to the yard and watched him hot-wire the Camaro. His hands had been so shaky and sweaty, it was a wonder he managed it. But Sam apparently liked what he saw and offered Billy a job as his "assistant."

Ever since that night, Billy worked for Sam. His cut wasn't much and the work was spotty, but the job left him with lots of free time to watch movies and tune up the Mustang and learn from Sam. Getting caught that night was definitely the best thing that ever happened to Billy Suggs, and he'd do most anything to keep from letting Sam down.

The storage place was set back from the street, out of range of the streetlights, and Billy was almost past before he saw it back there in the dark. He wheeled the Mustang into the parking lot, let it crawl forward until it was even with unit twenty-three, then killed the headlights. He was tempted to gun the engine a little, make sure Sam could hear him out here, but that kind of showboating made Sam frown. He'd said wait, so Billy would wait.

Sure enough, the garage door rolled up and there stood Sam, his blond hair glinting in the moonlight, his craggy face in shadow. He was dressed all in black, nearly invisible against the deeper black of the unit's interior. There was a car in there, but Billy couldn't tell much about it.

Sam crooked a finger at Billy, who popped open his car door.

"Leave it running," Sam said, his voice low. "This'll only take a minute."

Billy joined Sam outside the garage and watched as Sam let a flashlight dance over the parked car. He recognized it immediately as a 1965 Thunderbird, the type with the wide taillights that go all the way across the back. Turn on the blinker and the lights illuminated sequentially from inside to out: 1-2-3-4. 1-2-3-4.

"Gold flake, huh?" Billy said. "Cool. Just like Matt Helm."

"What?"

"Matt Helm. Spy movies starring Dean Martin? Drove one of

these. Dino always in the curved back seat with a couple of big-chested women—"

"Not now, Billy."

Billy clammed up. Sam looked around the parking lot, and he did the same, though he could see at a glance that nobody was around. Except for the surf-like whoosh of cars on San Mateo, the night was silent and empty.

"Want to show you something," Sam said. "Just so you'll know what we're up against."

A hundred questions danced through Billy's mind, but he said nothing. Another lesson he slowly was learning from Sam: Talk only when you've got something to say.

He grinned as Sam unlocked the trunk of the T-Bird. No telling what Sam might have in there. He was a prankster, always pulling jokes on people. Like Bruno, that three-hundred-pound biker at Mitch's, the one who was scared shitless of snakes. That time Sam draped the rubber snake over his bike's exhaust pipe, old Bruno had danced around, squealing like a schoolgirl. Billy thought he'd bust a gut laughing. Still a wonder Bruno hadn't taken a wrench to Sam's head, he was so mad. But Sam just grinned at him, acted innocent, and pretty soon even Bruno was laughing his ass off.

So, Billy's thinking about practical jokes, and Sam motions him over to the trunk and lifts the lid and there's a dead guy in there, dried blood all over him, and Billy almost starts laughing before he realizes, Jesus Christ, the guy really *is* dead. Before he could shout or run or something, Sam shut the lid and grabbed Billy by the arm.

"Sorry," he said. "Should've warned you. Pretty ugly, huh?"

"Fuck me, Sam. That guy, he's—"

"Shot in the face. And somebody set me up to find him."

Before Billy could think of a reply, Sam was rolling down the overhead door and putting a padlock through the loop down at the ground.

"The guy was in the trunk when you boosted the car?"

"What did you think? That I shot him?"

"No, Sam, nothing like that. But—"

"His cell phone was in there with him. It kept ringing, so I had to open the trunk. Good thing I did, too. Though it would've been better if it happened when there wasn't a cop around."

"Cop?"

"I'll tell you about it in the car."

Billy's heart pounded in his chest and he felt light-headed. The hell was he getting into? Boosting cars was one thing, but murder, shit, that was something else.

"You okay?" Sam asked.

"Just surprised. A dead guy—"

"Imagine how I felt. Let's go. We need to get far away from here."

"Damned straight."

They were miles away, on their way to Billy's place near the University of New Mexico, by the time Sam finished telling him about finding the body, the cop at the 7-Eleven, that the dead guy was wearing a wire.

Billy's head swam with all this new information. He caught himself tapping the steering wheel.

"So who do you think put him in there?" he asked.

"Don't know. The boost came from Robin, and the client supplied the key. I need to talk to her, find out who placed the order. I'm guessing that'll be our guy."

"But why would he *do* that?"

"Maybe he wanted me to find it," Sam said. "Or, maybe he had cops waiting for me somewhere, all ready to search the car."

"What you gonna do with that T-Bird?"

"I don't know yet. We can't leave it there long. Guy's already been dead a day or two. Somebody'll notice the smell."

"We should take that car out to the West Mesa and torch it," Billy said. "Out in the middle of the desert. Nobody'll find it there and, if they do, all the evidence will be burned up."

"I thought of that," Sam said, "but I want to poke around first, find out exactly what's going on. I don't want to drive that car anywhere until I'm sure it's safe."

The whole thing gave Billy the jitters, but he tried not to let on. If Sam thought it was okay to leave the body locked in the storage unit for another day or two, he probably knew best.

"What happens now?" Billy asked.

"Soon as we get to your place, I'll call Robin, see what she knows."

"Think she's still at the shop?"

"She's always at the shop."

"Call her on your cell."

"Somebody might be listening in. Let's just go to your place and call from there."

"Whatever you say, Sam."

Billy quick-shifted the Mustang into third, let the engine unwind a little before remembering to stay at the speed limit. Stick to the rules, Sam always said, and that applied now more than ever.

4

ROBIN MITCHELL STOOD in the open doorway of a work bay at her auto salvage shop, her hands on her hips, watching the police sort through carburetors and wheel rims and exhaust pipes. A fat uniformed cop dropped a bumper and it clanged loudly against the concrete floor.

"You chip that chrome," Robin said tightly, "and the city will be getting a bill from me."

The fat cop blushed, but his boss, Lieutenant Vic Stanton, gave Robin a look that said "shut up." She glared at him.

Stanton, that jerk, had given Robin's dad trouble for years. Always showing up unannounced, searching the place, *knowing* he'd find evidence of stolen vehicles. And, of course, he never found a thing. Mitch kept his chop shops well hidden, and he regularly gave up on a location and moved everything somewhere else, though it made his people bitch and moan. Here at the whitewashed garage just inside the city limits on South Broadway, everything was kept on the up-and-up.

Robin, who'd hung around the garage since she was in diapers, knew how careful her father had been, and she'd followed suit in the year since his death. Every junker, every part, every Vehicle Identification Number, was legal and above-board. Her records were up-to-date, and it would take a top-notch hacker to find anything illegal in her carefully camouflaged computer files.

The lieutenant didn't have a search warrant, but Robin was so confident, she'd told him to go ahead, knock himself out. He'd already made two circuits of the fenced two-acre lot out back, checking every car, shining a flashlight in the windows, and ordering Robin to open trunks and hoods. And he hadn't found a thing.

She could see desperation rising in Stanton's watery blue eyes. Against his red-veined skin, the eyes were like two lakes on a road map.

Robin put Stanton in his fifties, probably an alcoholic, undoubtedly divorced a time or two. Enough years in to retire, but nothing to live for but being a cop, throwing his weight around the Auto Theft Division. He kept the jacket of his tan suit buttoned, trying to hide his potbelly as he ordered his men around. The khaki suit and his steel-gray flattop made her think of drill sergeants.

"You about done here, Lieutenant?"

"I'll tell you when we're done," he said. "You just stand over there and keep your trap shut."

"Don't you guys have anything better to do than to harass an honest businesswoman? Shouldn't you be home, watching *Monday Night Football?*"

The fat cop, back there behind Stanton, rolled his eyes. Robin guessed that was exactly where he'd rather be.

"If you'd tell me what you're looking for, maybe I could help," she said, faking a smile. "I know where everything's kept."

"I'll bet you do," Stanton said gruffly.

"But, of course," she said, keeping her voice sweet, "since you didn't bring a *warrant*, I've got no information to go on."

The fat cop snickered, and Stanton shot him a look. Tubby got busy again, lifting stuff and looking under it. The police were wrecking the place without causing any actual damage, moving stuff around, getting parts out of sequence. It would take her crew days to put everything back together.

The garage's four work bays were lined with shelves and pegboards holding parts sorted and inventoried and ready for shipment. Attached to one side was Robin's office, just big enough for a couple of desks, some file cabinets, and an old sofa. Using state-of-the-art computers, she kept track of dozens of cars and hundreds of parts, with more moving in and out every day.

The other plainclothes officer, a well-dressed young man who'd identified himself as Sergeant Rey Delgado, came through the back door, brushing at the sleeves of his blue blazer. Delgado and two other cops had gone through the salvage yard again, covering the same ground she'd covered with the lieutenant. He caught Stanton's attention and shook his head. Delgado's dark eyes swept over to Robin, but he glanced away when he found her watching him. His cheeks colored, and Robin guessed he would've stared longer if she hadn't caught him looking.

She tossed her long black hair back over her shoulders and took two steps toward Stanton.

"You're finished?"

"Guess so," Stanton grumbled. "Should've known we wouldn't find anything. Otherwise, you wouldn't have let us search the place."

"I've got nothing to hide."

"Not here. But I'm guessing this isn't your only location. Your old man always kept cars scattered all over town, parked in people's back yards, hidden in garages."

She batted her eyes at him. "I don't know what you mean."

Stanton's face flushed. "The hell you don't. Your old man fenced hot cars and ran chop shops for years in this town, and I'd bet you're doing the same."

Robin tilted her head back, pointed her chin at Stanton.

"You got something on me, bring charges," she said. "You don't, then you'd better watch what you say. That sounds like slander to me."

Stanton's face got even redder. Beyond him, she could see Delgado tucking his chin. Looked like he was trying not to laugh.

"I'll say whatever I damned well please," Stanton said. "Screw around with me, and you'll be downtown so quick, you won't know what hit you."

"On what charge? Or doesn't APD believe in due process anymore?"

"I'll give you due process. Keep giving me lip, and I'll make you and your car thieves my full-time job."

"I thought auto theft *was* your full-time job."

Stanton got in her face, his face glowing red. His breath smelled of peppermint and stale beer.

"You're just like your old man. Always with the lip. Always think you can get away with any goddamned thing you want."

"I'm just running a business," she said. "One that you've disrupted for no apparent reason."

"You want a reason? We got a tip. Came from the DEA."

That surprised her. "You're looking for drugs?"

"Never mind what we're hunting. But let me ask you something: What do you hear these days from your old friend Sam Hill?"

Robin kept her face impassive. "Sam who?"

Stanton clenched his jaw and turned away from her. "Let's get the hell out of here."

He marched out to where the patrol cars were parked. The other cops trailed behind him, looking deflated.

The handsome cop, Delgado, paused as he passed Robin, and said, "Sorry about the mess."

She looked at him sharply, but saw he meant it, and grinned at him.

"Cost of doing business," she said. "I'll get it cleaned up."

He gave her a shy smile, then followed his boss out into the night.

Robin stood in the doorway, her hands tucked into the pockets of her jeans to protect them from the cold, until the last cop car had disappeared from sight on South Broadway. Then she went into the office and dialed Sam's number.

"Hey, I was just going to call you," he said. "But not on my cell phone. You at the shop?"

"Yeah. The cops were just here."

"Don't say anything else. Get to a pay phone. Call me at Billy's."

She hung up. Took a deep breath and blew it out. Stanton had asked about Sam by name, which was a bad sign.

What had Sam gotten into now? Stanton had said the tip came from the Drug Enforcement Administration. But that couldn't have anything to do with Sam. He wouldn't get involved with drug trafficking, not ever. Only thing he seemed to care about was cars.

Robin sometimes wished she understood Sam better. She often wondered what was going through his mind. Something about the way his mouth turned up at the corners, perpetually on the verge of an impish smile. He always seemed to be thinking of some joke.

This time, she thought, the joke may be on him.

5

SAM LOOKED AROUND Billy's tiny living room. Orange shag carpet, a gut-sprung sofa against one wall, a thrift-store lamp on a milk crate doing duty as an end table. The apartment was south of UNM, in an area known as the Student Ghetto, and Billy had embraced the college decorating scheme, though he'd never finished high school.

There were some differences from the typical student apartment. The wide-screen TV, one of Billy's first purchases when he started making dough from Sam. The posters on the wall, which featured Ferraris and a '66 Corvette rather than ballplayers or bands. The shelves full of videos instead of textbooks.

Billy was a Hollywood hound, crazy for movies, his only other passion besides cars. Sam didn't get it. He rarely went to the movies and hardly ever turned on his TV at home. He preferred books, or blues music on his state-of-the-art Sony stereo. Or, best yet, getting outdoors somewhere, hiking the crest of the Sandia Mountains or prowling the desert in search of Indian ruins. What's the point of living the thief's life, avoiding offices and regular jobs, if you're cooped up indoors all the time?

Billy hovered in the kitchen doorway, twitchy as a hamster. When Sam first met the youngster, he'd worried Billy Suggs was too nervous to be a car thief or to even work with one. But Billy, for all his physical symptoms, was cool on the inside, and that was good enough for Sam.

"You want a beer or something?"

"Got some in the fridge?"

Billy's smile winked on and off. "Of course."

"That's right. You're legal now, aren't you? Twenty-one years old. Can buy beer without getting some wino to front it for you."

Billy gave him a look. "You want a beer or not?"

"Sure."

His host scooted into the kitchen. Sam settled into the ratty armchair and tipped his head back. His shoulders cramped from tension and he stretched his arms over his head and twisted his neck around, trying to relieve the pressure. Finding a stiff can tie a man up in knots.

Billy came back into the living room, carrying two dark bottles of Dos Equis. Sam's favorite brand. The kid was learning.

Sam downed half the bottle and smacked his lips. "Thanks, partner. Just what I needed."

Billy perched on the edge of the grungy sofa, leaning forward, holding his bottle between his bony knees. His pointy chin was slightly off center, always made Sam think of a check mark. Billy was short and slight, looked like a skeleton with pale skin stretched tight over the bones. Sam could see his ribs where his shirt hung open. It made him think of the skinny frame of the dead junkie, Antonio Armas.

"So," Billy said as he ran a hand through his lank brown hair, "we just sit here now, wait for Robin to call back?"

"Don't know what else we'd do. Until I talk to her, I don't—"

The black telephone beside Sam's chair rang, and he snatched up the receiver.

"Sam?"

"Hi there. You at a pay phone?"

"Yeah, outside a burger joint. We need to make this quick. I'm freezing."

"I've got a little problem," he said.

"Does it have something to do with Lieutenant Stanton of the APD?"

"That who came to see you?"

"He and his boys ransacked the garage, looking for something. It'll take me days to put everything back where it belongs."

"Jesus. That explains a lot."

"What are you talking about?"

"That order you placed? The Thunderbird?"

"Yeah?"

"Had a little something extra in the trunk."

"Like what?"

"A dead guy."

A long pause. A corpse in a hot car was a new wrinkle.

"So that's what they were looking for," Robin said finally. "Stanton said the DEA had tipped them off to something, but he wouldn't say what."

"That fits. The dead guy's a junkie. And he's wired. I'm guessing he's a snitch."

Sam felt heat rise within him. It was just as he feared. Somebody planted the corpse in the car, then called the cops so they'd be waiting for him when he got to Robin's shop. If he hadn't stopped for a soda and found the body himself, he'd be in jail right now.

"Stanton asked me if I'd heard from you lately."

"And what did you say?"

"'Sam who?'"

Sam smiled. Nobody, not even Stanton, could bulldoze Robin Mitchell. Sam had known her since she was in junior high and she'd always been a pistol. He'd watched her grow up, and he'd never worried whether Robin would make it in the world. In her case, it was the world that had better watch out.

"Good answer," he said. "The way things are going tonight, you might not want to admit knowing me for a long time to come."

Another pause. Sam heard a horn honk in the background.

"So what do we do now?" she said. "And make it quick. I'm freezing to death here."

"I need to know one thing," he said. "Who ordered the Thunderbird?"

"You never ask about the client."

"I've never found a corpse before."

"Bad news, Sam. I don't know who ordered the car. It was brokered."

"By whom?"

"Ernesto Morelos."

"That fat bastard. He didn't say who ordered it?"

"No, but he was very clear about one thing."

"What's that?"

"He wanted *you* to boost the car. Asked for you by name. Said it was your specialty. I should've known something was fishy."

"Not your fault. Seemed like a good boost. No reason to question it. I'm just lucky I found the stiff before the cops found me."

"You think Ernesto set you up?"

"He helped. I'll have to go have a talk with him."

"Lot of gangbangers hang around Ernesto's place."

"When I go see him, I'll be ready."

"What are you going to do now?"

He looked around the living room. Billy watched him so closely, it was as if he were studying Sam for a science project. Sam gave him a grin.

"Nothing more I can do tonight," he said. "I'll get Billy to drive me home."

"Think that's safe?"

"Probably. Don't worry about it. Go get warm."

"Watch your ass, Sam."

Sam hung up, thinking, I'd rather watch yours, Robin.

6

TUESDAY MORNING, before Sam even had his first cup of coffee, he was outside his North Valley condo, filling his hummingbird feeders with sugar-water.

The Pueblo-style compound was beautifully landscaped, and the residents paid a hefty fee each month to keep the mowers and trimmers working. Velvety Russian olive trees and purple-leaf plums and squat evergreen shrubs circled the pools of lawn that were kept sopping green nine months out of the year. It was a regular little Eden surrounded by the one-story adobe dwellings. And it fooled the hummers into thinking they were set for the winter.

Of course, he mused as he topped off the second feeder, if it weren't for me, the birds still would fly off to warmer climes. I've upset the balance, so now it's my responsibility to keep them fed.

An impatient bird whirred past his head, making him duck. One of these days, he thought, one of those little bastards will zoom right into my face, poke my eye with a long, sharp beak. That'll teach me to mess around with Mother Nature.

He pulled his flannel bathrobe tighter around his chest and padded back indoors to get warm. Inside, he paused before the living room's picture window, stamping his bare feet to get the feeling back in them, and watched a rust-colored rufous and a greenish broadtail buzzing around the feeders, dipping their nips into the plastic blooms.

Sam needed to feel like he was sustaining some life in the world right now. Better than his thoughts through the night, which had been all about death.

The aroma of coffee pulled him away from the window. He went to the kitchen and poured himself a cup, added two sugars. His own version of sugar-water, plus some caffeine to kick his sleepy brain into gear.

The kitchen was separated from the living room by a breakfast bar, and Sam sat on a stool there, facing the living room, where long shelves down one wall held a small TV and his stereo and his hundreds of records and books. The furniture was low and fat, and a brightly zigzagged Mexican rug covered part of the redbrick floor. A hallway veered off behind the kitchen to the bathroom and single bedroom. The place was small but comfortable, tidy and sunlit.

Sam yawned. He'd tossed and turned all night, worrying over his situation, and he was no closer to an answer. Who would want to set him up? And why would they kill some junkie to make it happen?

He had no answers beyond Ernesto Morelos, who'd brokered the theft of the Thunderbird. Morelos *had* to know the boost was part of a trick to nail Sam.

So, today's first order of business was to go brace Morelos. It wasn't a chore Sam wanted to tackle alone. Robin had been right when she said Morelos' salvage yard swarmed with gangbangers. Sam had once met Morelos' nephew, a hard case called Chuco, who had all the trappings of the Fourteenth Street gang—the 'do rag, the baggy carpenter jeans, the tattoos on his neck, the hard glitter in his eyes. Kid couldn't be much more than twenty, but he already looked like someone who'd pulled hard time in a penitentiary. Sam knew for sure Chuco hung out at his uncle's shop. And where you find one modern-day gangster, you're sure to find others.

Ernesto Morelos might've been a Fourteenth Streeter himself back in the day when gangs were all about fistfights and low-riders, rather than crack and turf and guns. Now, Ernesto must be close to sixty, fat and bald and worn out. Small wonder he kept young toughs around to protect his business.

Sam had dealt with Ernesto as little as possible over the years, though their paths crossed from time to time. Mitch had always considered Ernesto a small-timer, dealing junkers to Old Mexico when the real money was in chop-shop parts.

Take a car like an Oldsmobile Cutlass. Popular and easy to steal. General Motors made few changes to the car over its production life, which meant many of the parts were interchangeable. Guy needs an alternator for, say, a '95 Cutlass, he doesn't care if the refurbished one he buys came from a '94, as long as it fits. Mitch's boys would strip every useable part off a boosted Cutlass, from the engine block to the hubcaps. Clean them up, catalog them, resell them for half the price of new factory parts.

"See," Mitch liked to say around his ever-present cigar, "we're good citizens. We're *recycling*."

One of Morelos' boys boosts the same car, Ernesto wouldn't chop it up. Too much work. Instead, he'd dummy up a fresh paper trail to show that he bought it used from out of state. Then that car, along with two or three others, would be chained together into a wagon train of hot steel and towed to the Mexican border. Sell the whole car for twice what it was worth to some *campesino* who didn't know any better.

Visit border towns, and you see old American cars all over the place. On the outskirts of those towns, you'll find hundreds of rusting hulks, abandoned when they went to shit and their owners couldn't find or afford parts for them.

Ernesto wasn't much more than a junkman. He merely dealt his junk across an international border. Sam had seen those caravans on back roads in New Mexico, traveling way over the speed limit, too much weight behind each tow rig to stop if some farmer pulled out in front of them in his pickup. Every year, four or five people got croaked in such accidents. Sam imagined that Ernesto Morelos was too busy raking in money to give a shit about things like life and death.

Sitting at the counter, thinking about Morelos, Sam worked up a pretty good rage. He'd go see Ernesto all right, and he wouldn't be gentle with his questions. He'd take his pal Way-Way with him. One look at Way-Way, and the gangbangers would go find somebody else to fight.

Sam glanced at the clock on the wall. Too early to call Way-Way, who worked as a bouncer at The Tropics nightclub downtown. Wake him before noon, and Way-Way would never stop bitching. Still, Sam should get a shower and get into his clothes. Be ready when the time comes.

His doorbell rang. The hell could that be?

He adjusted his robe as he went to the door. Looked through the peephole, saw a sleek-haired guy in a blue suit and a tan overcoat. He didn't recognize him, but he opened the door and said, "Yeah?"

"Sam Hill?"

Uh-oh. The voice of authority.

"Who are you?"

"Sergeant Rey Delgado. APD Auto Theft Division."

The cop pulled a thin wallet from his inside pocket and flipped it open to show his gold badge. Sam glanced past him, saw another plainclothes man standing on the lawn beyond.

"One of my neighbors lose a car?"

"No, sir. We'd like to talk with you. Downtown. You might want to get dressed first."

Sam got a sinking feeling inside his chest. "Am I under arrest?"

"Just a friendly talk. We think you could help in one of our investigations."

Delgado didn't look particularly friendly. The Auto Theft Division meant Lieutenant Vic Stanton, and there was nothing whatsoever friendly about him.

Stanton had tried to catch Sam for years. This wasn't the first time he'd been summoned to headquarters for a "talk." But Stanton never managed to make a charge stick, which probably kept him awake nights.

"This isn't a good time for me," Sam said. "Why don't we make an appointment for me come down and see you?"

Delgado shook his head slightly. "Now would be best for us."

"Okay. Want me to drive myself down there?"

"You can ride with us. We'll bring you back when we're done."

Sam doubted that very much. More likely, they'd throw him in a cage until he could get hold of his attorney.

"Just let me get dressed," he said. "Wait here."

He closed the door on the sergeant and headed for his bathroom, pausing in the kitchen long enough to drain his coffee cup. Going to be a long morning, and the coffee at the cop shop sucked.

7

SAM DIDN'T NEED TO fret about the coffee at police headquarters. He wasn't offered any. Delgado took him directly upstairs, put him in a puke-beige interrogation room and left him there.

The room was furnished with a gray metal table and three matching steel chairs. Sam plunked onto one of the slatted chairs and tried to get comfortable. It was like sitting on a steam grate.

He knew they'd let him cool a while. Give him time to worry. He sat facing a large mirror set into the wall. Delgado and Stanton probably stood behind it, watching, waiting for Sam to start sweating. He resisted the urge to make faces at the men behind the mirror, and the stronger urge to moon them.

After fifteen minutes, Delgado entered the room, carrying a black tape recorder. Lieutenant Stanton came in right behind him, and shut the door.

"Mornin', scumbag," Stanton said. "Sergeant Delgado says he got you out of bed."

"I was up, but I was still working on my first cup of coffee."

"Sergeant Delgado said you made him wait outside while you took a shower and got dressed. Officer tells you you're going downtown, and you take a shower?"

"A quick one. Didn't know when I'd get another chance."

"You don't like the showers in the lockup?"

"I'm big on privacy."

Stanton let a smile ooze onto his face. "We'll just have to see about that, won't we?"

Sam straightened in the uncomfortable chair while Delgado fiddled with the knobs on the tape recorder.

"You want to tell me what this is about?" Sam asked.

"All in good time." Stanton perched on the remaining chair, and lifted his chin at Delgado to show he was ready to start. As preliminaries go, Sam thought, that wasn't bad. A little casual verbal abuse. Better than getting slapped around.

Stanton looked back over his shoulder at the mirror, then scooted his chair over a few inches to his left. Ah, Sam thought, video camera working behind the glass. Before he had a chance to wonder about it, Delgado said for the benefit of the tape recorder, "Interrogation with Sam Hill. Tuesday, November 12, 9:27 a.m. Present are Sergeant Rey Delgado and Lieutenant Vic Stanton."

Delgado watched the reels of the cassette tape, making sure everything was working, then he raised his head and focused on Sam.

"Your name is Sam Hill, no middle initial?"

"That's right."

The corners of Delgado's mouth turned up. "What kind of person names his kid Sam Hill?"

"My old man had a sense of humor. Runs in the family. His name was Bunker Hill."

"Or, 'Bunco,' as we all called him," Stanton said. "Small-time grifter, worked the short con. He was an optimist—always wore a slouch hat and a raincoat, out here in the desert. You an optimist, Sam?"

"I'm an opportunist."

"Nice. That's some way to live. Preying on others, just like your old man. How long has he been dead now?"

"Couple of years."

"Died up at the pen in Santa Fe, didn't he?"

"That's right. A stroke."

"And your mom was a lush, as I recall. You were just a kid when she drank herself to death."

Sam stared at him, said nothing.

"It's like I told you before, Rey," Stanton said. "Crime runs in families, just like alcoholism. It's genetic, like the color of your hair or the shape of your face."

Stanton sat back and pressed his thin lips together, ready to let the sergeant take over again, now that he'd needled Sam about his parentage. Delgado got a few more of the preliminaries out of the way—Sam's address, his Social Security number, his date of birth thirty-seven years ago. Then he asked, "What do you do for a living, Mr. Hill?"

"I'm an investor."

That made Stanton snort. Delgado ignored him.

"What kind of investments?"

"Stocks, bonds, mutual funds, stuff like that. I work at home."

"A day trader?"

"Not exactly. I don't like to work that hard. I just manage my money."

Delgado paused, then said, "Must've taken quite a stake to get started. Where did that money come from?"

"An inheritance. From my father."

"Now that's bullshit," Stanton exclaimed. "Old Bunco never had two dimes to rub together his whole life."

Sam raised a shoulder and let it drop. Said nothing.

"You ever been arrested, Mr. Hill?" Delgado asked. "Ever done time?"

"Not since I was a juvie. Twenty years ago."

"That's right. I saw in your file that you pulled a year at the boys' school at Springer. Auto theft, right?"

"Joy-riding," Sam said. "A youthful mistake."

"Mm-hm. But nothing since?"

"Not even a speeding ticket."

Delgado sat back in his chair, let the smile dance around his lips. "Guess that makes you a good citizen, doesn't it, Mr. Hill?"

"If you say so."

"As a good citizen, it's probably in your best interest to cooperate with police investigations."

"Depends."

"But you've got nothing to hide, right?"

"Everybody's got something to hide. Even you, Sergeant."

Delgado's cheeks colored slightly, but he didn't take the bait. "Where were you last night, Mr. Hill?"

"Home."

"That's funny. We sent a couple of officers by your house. They rang the bell. Nobody answered."

"I didn't hear it. Did they see my car out front?"

"As a matter of fact, they did. But that doesn't mean much in your case, does it?"

"I don't know what you mean."

"You drive lots of different cars, right?"

"Just the one. Five-year-old Chevy Caprice, legally registered in my name."

"You weren't driving a different vehicle last night?"

"Nope. Like I said, I was at home. Maybe they knocked while I was in the shower."

"We called a couple of times. You didn't answer the phone."

"It was a long shower."

Stanton muttered, "Take more than a shower to get the dirt off you."

"What was that, Lieutenant?" Sam said. "You need to speak up if we're going to get you on the record."

"Screw you. You hear that all right?"

"Loud and clear."

Delgado shot Stanton a disapproving look, but said nothing to him. Instead, he asked Sam, "Ever hear of a man named Antonio Armas?"

"No."

"Sure about that? You might want to think about it before you answer."

"Never heard of him. Who is he?"

"An informant for the DEA. He's been missing for three days."

"Too bad. Must be dangerous being a rat."

"We were told you knew where he was," Delgado said.

"Who told you that?"

Delgado smiled thinly.

"All right, you don't have to tell me," Sam said. "But whoever it is, they're full of shit. I don't know any DEA informants. And I for sure don't know this Antonio Whoever."

"Armas."

"Don't know him."

Delgado and Stanton swapped a look, but Sam couldn't tell where they were headed next.

"Why, do you suppose, would we get such a tip?" Delgado asked finally. "This information was very specific. Said Sam Hill was involved, that he knew where to find Armas."

"Maybe you got the wrong Sam Hill."

"How many could there be?"

Sam shrugged.

"What about a gold 1965 Thunderbird, belongs to a lawyer named Timothy Blankenship?"

"Don't know him either. Or his car."

"Blankenship reported the car stolen last night," Delgado said.

"Too bad. But not my problem."

Stanton leaned forward in his chair, his gray hair bristling, a flush rising in his face.

"Your problem is whatever I say it is, shitbird. We got good information here, and if you think you can dance around us, you're even more full of it than your old man was."

Sam felt the muscles in his jaw twitching. Stanton kept dragging his father into this, trying to get a rise out of him. Sam needed to tread carefully, not let the anger swell up inside. An outburst was just what Stanton wanted.

"I told you I know nothing about it," he said evenly.

"You know something," Stanton barked. "You just think you're smart. You're not, buddy. Just because I haven't locked you up before doesn't mean I don't know all about you. You're a car thief. Working with Mitchell all these years."

"Mitchell?"

"Buford Mitchell, a.k.a 'Mitch,' of Mitch's Auto Salvage. You gonna tell me you've never heard of him either?"

Sam grinned. "Place down on South Broadway? I think I bought a carburetor from him once."

"Aw, horseshit. This guy's impossible."

Stanton threw himself back in his chair, nearly tipped it over. Sam glanced at the mirror, then turned his attention back to Delgado.

"If you're so sure of your answers," the sergeant said, "maybe you wouldn't mind taking a polygraph test."

Sam didn't even pause to think it over. "I'd mind it very much.

Everyone knows polygraphs are worthless. You guys could make that machine say I was lying, no matter what I told you."

"If you've got nothing to hide—"

"I'm not taking a lie detector test. In fact, I don't want to answer any more questions. I think it's time to call my lawyer."

"But you're not under arrest."

"I don't get a phone call? You brought me down here against my will, poking around, trying to entrap me. Now I don't get a lawyer?"

"All right," Delgado said brusquely. "Who's your attorney?"

"Lorena Alvarado."

Delgado and Stanton looked at each other, their faces twisted up like somebody had farted.

Sam said, "I see you know her."

8

AN HOUR LATER, Sam exited the cop shop with his attorney. Lorena Alvarado stood five feet tall and weighed two hundred pounds, most of it around her hips. With her jowls and undershot jaw, she looked like a bulldog wearing gold-rimmed glasses. Had a bulldog's fierce personality, too. Sam often thought she should wear a sign saying, "Beware of Lawyer."

"Thanks for getting here so quickly," he said.

Lorena dug around in her leather handbag, came up with a thin brown cigarette. She clamped it between her teeth and torched the end of it with a Bic lighter, then pulled her overcoat tighter around her bulging body. A sharp wind riffled her short black hair.

"No problem," she said, smoke trailing out her snout. "I was across the street at Metro Court when I got the message. Soon as I got done there, I trotted over to rescue you."

Sam couldn't imagine Lorena "trotting" anywhere, but he said, "You sure put the whammy on Stanton."

"That jerk wouldn't know due process if it bit him on the ass. You'd think a guy like that, been on the force for decades, would've figured it out by now."

"He thinks the law is whatever he says it is."

"Still, he knows he can't hold you unless he's pressing charges."

"Said I was a 'material witness.'"

"My fat ass. What did you supposedly witness?"

"They were asking about some DEA informant who's missing. Guy named Antonio Armas. Ever hear of him?"

Lorena shook her head and belched more smoke. "Why would they tie him to you?"

"They were cagey about it. Said they got a tip, but they wouldn't say from whom. When I heard that, I told them I wanted my attorney."

"Good call. You answer any of their questions?"

"Just the basics. Name, rank, and serial number."

"Nothing else?"

"No. Why?"

"I've known you since grade school, Sam. You've never been able to keep your mouth shut. You're too busy being clever."

"Not this time."

"You didn't know what they were talking about?"

Sam shook his head, but he felt himself grinning.

"Shit, don't say anything else," she said. "I don't want to know the details. Not until I need them in court."

"We're not going to court. You sprung me already."

"You saw how Stanton reacted. He'll haul your butt in again."

"No doubt. But I'm in the clear for now."

Lorena sighed. Dropped her cigarette to the sidewalk and ground it out with an expensive-looking pointy shoe.

"When they come for you again, don't say *anything*. Just clam up. For once in your life."

"You bet."

She looked at the lowering gray clouds, then glanced up and down the street. A few low-lifes hung around outside the doors of Metro Court, smoking and stamping against the chill. Cops came and went through the glass doors of headquarters.

"Colder than an Eskimo's ass out here," she said. "And I've got an arraignment coming up in ten minutes across the street."

"Another trumped-up charge?"

"Hardly. Guy is guilty as sin. Wife-beater. I hate the bastard, but he'll get his day in court."

"He hired a good-looking woman attorney to try to sway the judge?"

Lorena rolled her eyes.

"Don't be clever, Sam. Go home. And try to stay out of trouble."

"Will do. Thanks again."

"Keep your thanks. You'll be getting my bill. Pay it in a timely fashion."

"Always do."

"Bye, Sam." Lorena turned and waddled across the street.

Sam watched until she was safely through the doors of Metro Court. Then he pulled his cell phone from his jacket pocket and called Billy. Once Lorena had chewed on them, the cops had forgotten their promise to give Sam a ride home.

9

BILLY SUGGS SPOTTED Sam standing outside the cop shop when he still was two blocks away. Sam paced near the curb, his breath fogging before him, his shoulders hunched under his leather jacket. The wind swirled grit and litter around his feet.

Billy stopped the Mustang right in front of Sam, who quickly popped open the door.

"Get in before you freeze to death."

"Thanks, Billy. Glad you were available. I would've turned into a Popsicle waiting for a cab."

Sam could've gone indoors to warm up, either at the cop shop or across the street at the courthouse, but Billy understood why that hadn't been an option. Better to freeze.

"Always available for you, Sam. And it's William now."

"What?"

"I want people to start calling me William."

Sam rubbed at his wind-reddened nose and squinted at Billy, who put the Mustang in gear and steered into traffic.

"Why the hell would you want to be called that?"

"Sounds more serious. I think people will take me seriously if I'm William instead of Billy."

Sam thought it over. "William sounds more grown-up?"

"You could say that. I'm twenty-one now. I need to start acting like a man."

"Plenty of men named Billy."

"Yeah, but are they men you'd admire?"

"Oh, you want admiration now?"

"I mean, would you take them seriously?"

"Billy Martin. Billy Bob Thornton. Billy Graham."

"Yeah, sure, them."

"Billy goat. Billy club."

"See what I mean?"

"Yeah, but why William? William sounds like somebody who's trying to sell you insurance."

"It's my name. Lot of famous people named William. Serious people. William Shakespeare. William Holden. William the Conqueror."

"William the *Conqueror*?"

"Saw it in a movie."

"Why don't you just go by Bill?"

"I don't like that. Sounds like something you owe."

"Bill Clinton."

"That's another reason."

"You could double up, like that actor, Billy Dee Williams. Have it both ways."

"Just call me William, okay?"

"All right, Billy. Sure."

Billy sighed. He knew Sam would give him a raft of shit when he told him about the name change, but he hadn't expected it to go on this long.

"Where are we going anyway? Your place?"

"That would be great, *William*. The cops told me they'd give me a ride home, but we see how that went."

"Speaking of which, you gonna tell me what they wanted? All you said on the phone was they had some questions for you."

"They had questions all right. All about the guy in the T-Bird. Somebody tipped them that I knew what happened to him."

"What kind of rat would do that?"

"I don't know, but I plan to find out."

They drove in silence as the Mustang passed Old Town, Albuquerque's adobe tourist zone, the parking lot full of Winnebagos and bland rent-a-cars. Billy stopped for the light at Rio Grande Boulevard, his blinker going. He revved the engine, impatient to get going.

"Relax," Sam said. "We're in no hurry. Unless you've got plans to go conquer something."

Billy glared at him, but Sam grinned until Billy relaxed.

"Asshole."

"You want people to take you seriously, you should clean up your language."

"Fuck that. What are you gonna do now, Sam?"

"Talk to Ernesto Morelos. He set up the boost for somebody, and I'm guessing that somebody is the one who clipped Armas."

"Want me to go with you?"

"No. Morelos surrounds himself with bad boys. It could get rough."

"I don't mind rough."

Sam looked him up and down. Billy gripped the wheel tighter, trying to make the muscles in his skinny arms bulge.

"I'm taking Way-Way," Sam said. "But stay near a phone in case we need you."

"All right."

"Hey, there's another example for you. Way-Way. Goes around with a goofy name like that, yet everybody takes him seriously."

"Hell, yeah. He weighs, like, three hundred pounds. Looks like Attila the Hun. I guess people would take him seriously."

Sam laughed. "If they want to keep breathing, they do."

"I don't have that kind of physical presence."

"*Physical presence*? Where you getting this stuff?"

"Movies."

"Figures."

The light changed. Billy steered onto five-lane Rio Grande Boulevard, passed a slow-moving pickup. Out of habit, he checked his rear-view mirror.

"Uh-oh."

"What?"

"We got company."

"You hear that in a movie, too?" Sam said as he turned in the seat to look behind them.

"Heard it in about a thousand movies. See the black Crown Vic?"

"Probably a couple of Stanton's boys. He's really got a hard-on for me."

"What did you ever do to him?"

"Boosted cars. He doesn't like that."

"Some people are so narrow-minded."

As they neared Sam's condo, he told Billy to go ahead and turn in.

"Just drop me at the door and then get out of here. No telling what they've got planned for me."

"You got it, Sam."

Billy turned into the driveway of the lushly landscaped condos and bounced over a couple of speed bumps on his way to Sam's door. No sign of the unmarked cop car behind them.

"Thanks for the ride," Sam said as he opened his door.

"Sure you don't want me to stick around?"

"Later. William."

Sam climbed out into the cold, then hurried around the front end of the Mustang toward his home. Billy put the car in gear and let it creep away. The asphalt made a circle around the huddled condos, and Billy followed it all the way around, glancing at his mirrors, waiting for the Crown Vic to show up.

As soon as he turned back onto Rio Grande, headed for home, he spotted the black car behind him again. He hadn't gone three blocks before red and blue lights began flashing behind the grille.

"Aw, shit." He plucked his cell phone from his pocket and hit the speed-dial.

"Hello?"

"Sam, it's Billy."

"Thought it was William now."

"Screw you. Your cop buddies are pulling me over. Looks like I'm going downtown, too."

"Damn. Sorry, Billy. I should've called that cab."

Billy turned on his blinker and pulled off onto a side street, the Crown Vic right behind him.

"How do you want me to play it?"

"Just keep your mouth shut. I'll get my attorney over there to spring you, quick as I can. Her name's Lorena Alvarado."

"You've mentioned her."

"She's scary as hell, but she'll take good care of you."

"Okay, Sam. Here they come."

He watched in the mirrors as two suits climbed out of the Crown Vic.

"Hang up, Billy. And keep your hands in plain sight. You don't want to be an APD *accident*."

Billy tossed the phone on the seat beside him. He put both hands on the wheel and waited for the tap on his window.

10

TWENTY MINUTES LATER, Sam got off the phone with Lorena Alvarado's secretary, cursing over the delays. The secretary said her boss was in court, and it could be a while before she got the message about Billy being picked up. Sam didn't worry about Billy rolling over on him; the kid was tougher than he looked. But he didn't want Billy locked up, even briefly. Little mouse of a guy like Billy wouldn't stand up long against the drunken thugs and heartless homeboys who populated the Bernalillo County jail.

Worse, Billy had been hauled in through no fault of his own. The kid kept his nose clean, on Sam's orders. He'd laid down a lot of rules for Billy, dangling before him a lifestyle of low risk and high profit. And the kid had done his damnedest to play by those rules.

No, Billy had been picked up solely because of his connection to Sam. Lieutenant Stanton clearly thought he had something that would put him behind bars for good. He couldn't catch him boosting cars—Sam was too careful for that—so he'd use this other thing, this dead junkie, to finally nail him. And Stanton wasn't above using Billy, if he could figure a way to swing it.

Sam wondered briefly whether the lieutenant himself had set him up. Had he forced Ernesto Morelos to arrange for Sam to boost the T-Bird? Stanton could have something on Morelos, holding a charge over his head, making him play along. It wouldn't take much to sweat Ernesto.

But it just didn't figure. Sam and Stanton hadn't crossed paths in a couple of years. Why would the cop suddenly come after him? Plus, if it was Stanton, that would mean he was involved in the death of Antonio Armas, at least after the fact. No matter how much Sam would like to believe that, it didn't sound right. The lieutenant wasn't a dirty cop. He was just an asshole.

But if not Stanton, then who? Somebody had gone to a lot of trouble to link Sam to Armas. Apparently, the only one who might know whodunit was that dirt bag Ernesto Morelos.

Sam checked his watch. Still a little early to wake Way-Way.

He thought about calling Robin at the shop, but she wouldn't know anything new. And she'd sounded pissed the night before about the cops wrecking her place. He was trying very hard these days to stay on Robin's good side.

It wasn't always easy. Robin had inherited Mitch's fiery temper. The wetbacks and beefy bikers who worked for her had learned to tiptoe around the shop when she was angry. A couple had tried to push her around when she took over the business. Those guys now were swapping anecdotes in the unemployment line. And one, a tough guy called Tommy Cheeks, had spent time in intensive care after Robin laid a socket wrench upside his head.

Robin worried Sam. She'd graduated from the University of New Mexico with a degree in computer science and had worked several years for one of Albuquerque's many software companies. Since taking over Mitch's Auto Salvage, she'd found the Internet a great market for hard-to-find auto parts. Some car nut couldn't locate a taillight cover for his beloved '68 Chevelle SS, he'd search his computer until he turned one up at Mitch's. And he'd gladly pay twice the going rate to have it delivered straight to his home.

While that end of the business was booming, Sam's end—stealing special cars for special clients—mostly ran on inertia these days. Mitch had kept it up because, hell, he was a car nut, too. And he appreciated Sam's abilities. Some customer would tell Mitch he wanted a '71 Mustang fastback like the one he drove in high school. Sam would steal such a car and deliver it to Mitch, who'd lovingly restore and repaint it, give it a new identity, and sell it to the nostalgic client for thirty grand. Sam and Mitch make money, the client gets his car, insurance pays off the stiff who lost the Mustang. And if the poor victim wants a car like the one he lost, well, he should come see Mitch.

But since Mitch's death, a lot of the old clients had drifted away. Word gets around. Sam's income had gone into a tailspin.

Not that he needed much. He lived simply. His condo was paid for. He had money stashed in safety-deposit boxes in several banks around the state. He even had a few of the investments he'd mentioned to that cop, Delgado. Sam could steal two, three cars a month, collect a few grand on each of them, and get by just fine.

Now, with Stanton and his boys watching around the clock, Sam clearly needed to lie low for a while. He could afford to take a break, but what about Billy? The kid barely eked a living out of the twenty percent share Sam threw his way. If he couldn't send him any work, Billy would have to find something else, maybe even—God forbid—a regular job. Billy wasn't cut out for that. Like Sam, he needed the adrenaline rush that came from boosting cars. Neither did well just hanging around, killing time until the next score. They'd get twitchy, tired of waiting. Somebody could make a mistake.

Plus, the lull would give Robin one more reason to shut down the operation. If she went legit, where would that leave Sam? Out hawking his services on the street? Hey, buddy, can you spare some change for a mint-condition 1957 Buick?

Maybe it was time to hang the whole thing up. He'd thought a lot lately about going straight. He was nearly forty years old, for shit's sake. Wasn't it time he grew up, settled down, got a real career? But he didn't know anything else. And he didn't exactly have a resume that would interest potential employers.

Sam had considered finding another partner after Mitch died. But he and Robin were practically family. Mitch had certainly served as a father figure to Sam, more than his own father ever had been. Which meant, what, that Robin was his kid sister? That's the way he'd felt toward her when she was a leggy pony of a girl and he was nearly five years older, starting to make a go of it with Mitch. Then she'd gone off to UNM and Sam hadn't seen her much. She was busy with her studies and her sorority and her boyfriends, all suddenly more interesting than auto parts and grease monkeys. Then she'd been a busy career woman, engaged at least once, but never married, and he only saw her once in a while, maybe at Christmas or similar family gatherings at Mitch's house. Since she took over the business, they'd spent more time together, and Sam saw how she'd grown into a smart, sexy woman. He had trouble thinking of her in brotherly terms.

He felt a spark of attraction every time he saw her these days, though he'd never been bold enough to mention it. He thought she sensed it, too, but they'd kept everything strictly business so far. Probably for the best. You don't mix business with romance, especially their kind of business. Not unless you want to spend a lot of years writing to each other from separate prisons. And Mitch, no matter how much he'd loved Sam, would've never approved of his daughter taking up with a car thief.

Sam dated a lot of different women over the years, never getting too entangled, keeping much of his life secret from them. But lately there'd been no one else. Just Robin on his mind, all the damned time.

Robin got her dark good looks from her mother, a Garcia who still was striking in a matronly way, though she constantly wore black and spent all her time kneeling in church and counting her rosary beads. Loya Mitchell spent thirty years praying that her husband would stay out of prison, and now her daughter was in the same line of work. A wonder her knees hadn't worn out by now.

Robin had eyes like strong black coffee and a great white smile, when you could get it to emerge. Lately, Sam found himself spending too much time hanging around the shop, trying to make her smile.

If the cops kept riding him, he couldn't go near the garage, couldn't see Robin, couldn't make a living.

Anger boiled up within him. He had a good life, a quiet life. He did his best to avoid conflict, to not *bother* anyone—if you didn't count the poor schmucks whose cars he stole. Now, some ass-wipe had sicced the cops on him, and who knows how long they'd be watching him?

The only answer, at least in the short-term, was to make the Armas problem go away. Maybe then the cops would lay off. If not, Sam would need to make some decisions about his future. About a career. About Robin.

He put on his leather jacket and slipped out of the house. He checked the parking lot for cop cars, but saw none. He climbed into his four-door Chevy Caprice, a wide-assed white whale of a car so plain it was practically invisible. Under the hood, it was something else. Sam had special-ordered the "police interceptor package"—a powerful V-8 and four-barrel carb and heavy-duty suspension—and the car would outrun virtually anything he'd meet on the street.

He took it slow, though, on the drive to Way-Way's house downtown. Went miles out of his way on sudden detours, watching his mirrors the whole time, but never spotted a tail. Maybe the cops were busy sweating Billy. They didn't seem to be on Sam at the moment.

And that, considering what he planned to do, was a good thing.

11

WAYMON WAYNE HENDERSON lived in a white frame house within walking distance to his job at The Tropics, one of the dozen or so nightclubs that make Central Avenue a happening place on weekends. The Tropics was in an old office building, which the owner had gutted and redecorated. The club had a thatched ceiling and rattan ceiling fans and seascape murals and other island crap everywhere. The waitresses dressed like hula girls and the drinks came in coconuts with umbrellas sticking in them. Sam Hill didn't know how Way-Way could stand to spend every night there.

Way-Way's home, on the other hand, was devoid of ornamentation. No knickknacks. No family photos. No artwork on the peeling walls. Barely any furniture. Walk into the small, high-ceilinged living room, and you'd guess that no one lived there, that someone just used the place to store weight-lifting equipment.

The bare hardwood floors were dented and scarred from dropped barbells, and the centerpiece was a Universal multi-station lifting bench. Crunchy towels piled in one corner, fresh towels stacked in another.

As usual, the front door was unlocked, allowing Sam to waltz right in. Way-Way's reputation was such that no one would ever think to burglarize his home. If some unwitting junkie stumbled into the place, looking for something to steal, he'd find nothing worth having. Sam asked him about it once, saying maybe somebody'd steal his barbells. Way-Way had said, "Hell, if he's man enough to lift 'em, he can have 'em."

Deep snores rumbled from the bedroom. The big man worked until 3 a.m., then slept until noon. Spent the afternoon lifting and stretching and running. By the time he got back to work again at

6 p.m., he was so pumped up he could barely fit through the wide door of The Tropics. Only the drunkest of the drunk ever caused any trouble at the nightclub, and Way-Way could usually stifle that with one fierce shot of his patented bouncer's glare. But once in a while some yahoo made Way-Way earn his considerable paycheck. All those muscles came in handy for dragging unconscious drunks outside by their collars.

Sam knew all about Way-Way's schedule because he sometimes called on his old friend when he needed beef on a job. Usually, that meant somebody getting frisky over payment. One look at Way-Way—six-foot-seven, two-hundred-ninety pounds, maybe five percent body fat—tended to change their minds.

People rolled over so easily for Way-Way, he found it a little frustrating. Sam knew he missed football, though it had been fifteen years since he stepped onto a playing field. He missed the contact and the power and the speed. Another adrenaline junkie. Though Way-Way had a real job—more or less—he was always available for some action on the side, especially if it meant he might get to clobber somebody.

The kitchen had the bare essentials, but the refrigerator was empty as usual—Way-Way ate most of his meals for free at The Tropics. Sam found a can of coffee in a cupboard and set some to perking.

He poked around in the kitchen cabinets until he came up with two battered pans, then carried them into Way-Way's bedroom. The giant was flat on his back on the king-sized bed, only a sheet over his massive chest, though it was freezing in the house. His bare head needed shaving, and the stubble made his scalp look blue. Sunlight poured through flimsy curtains over two windows, hit him right in the face, but Way-Way was a heavy sleeper. His mouth, framed by an unruly black Fu Manchu mustache, hung open, emitting thunderous snores.

Sam stopped near the foot of the bed, took a deep breath and started banging the pans together like cymbals. Sounded like the end of the world, but Way-Way merely opened one eye. Then his brow creased into the scowl that kept order at The Tropics every night.

"Stop that."

Sam merrily whanged the pans together some more. He shouted over the noise, "Not 'til I'm sure you're awake."

"I'm awake."

Clang-clang.

"Sit up. I know you. You'll go right back to sleep."

Clang-clang.

"I said I'm awake."

Clang-clang.

"How about if I kill you? Would that prove it?"

Sam left off the clatter. He was wearing out anyway. He dropped his arms, let the pans dangle.

Way-Way sat up and rubbed at his face with hands the size of hubcaps.

"What time is it? And what the hell do you want?"

"It's noon. And I've got a job for you."

Way-Way fell back on his pillow, groaning.

"Want me to bang these pans some more? I've got a nifty version of 'Inna-Gadda-Da-Vida.'"

"Want me to pull your arms off?"

"Come on, get up. We got work to do."

"What kinda work?"

"Remember Ernesto Morelos? Always has those gangbangers hanging around his place?"

"Yeah." Way-Way's eyes were closed.

"How'd you like to hurt some of them?"

His eyes popped open. "Shit, man, why didn't you say so?"

Over coffee in the kitchen, Sam told Way-Way about the corpse in the trunk and the grilling by the cops. Way-Way wore only boxer shorts. He leaned his hips against the counter, kept his massive arms crossed over his naked chest, and his head bowed while he listened. Sam couldn't tell if Way-Way was staring at the floor or at the surgical scars that decorated both his knees. The ceramic coffee mug looked dainty as a teacup in his hand.

When Sam was done, Way-Way raised his head and looked at him. "You still got the body stashed away?"

"Yeah."

"Good thing we've had this cold snap."

"It won't last. But I want to figure out what's going on before I move the body."

"You think Ernesto set you up?"

"I think he helped."

"And we're gonna go see him now?"

"Soon as you get dressed."

"Give me five minutes."

Way-Way padded off to his bedroom and closed the door behind him. Sam drifted into the living room and examined the weights. Two hundred pounds on the barbells. The weight machine set at three hundred. Kid stuff for Way-Way. Sam thinking, I'd be lucky if I could *roll* that barbell across the room, much less lift it.

Way-Way was one of those pituitary cases who was oversized from the day he was born. Thirteen pounds at birth, nearly killed his poor mother. When he was six years old, he was already burly as a wrestler. A full-sized man at twelve, and he had a *mustache*. By junior high, it was clear Way-Way planned to just keep growing. He broke two hundred pounds, and it was all muscle. Two-fifty, and he still had enough hops to dunk a basketball. Two-eighty, and he could play offensive line all by himself.

College coaches started sniffing around when Way-Way was a sophomore. By the time he graduated from Albuquerque High, agents and scouts loitered in his lawn like hound dogs around a bitch in heat, praying for a chance to get at him. Good hometown boy that he was, Way-Way signed with the University of New Mexico, moved to defense, and spent four years lunching on quarterbacks, the only bright spot on a series of limpdick Lobo teams. He blew a knee his junior year, worked like a plow horse to come back. Finished a stellar senior year by blowing the other knee. And football was over.

Locals still recognized Way-Way on the street—hell, it was hard to miss him—and some would smile and shake his hand and clap him on his broad back. Sharing memories of his monster tackles on muddy Saturday afternoons. To them, he still was a hometown hero. Other folks, those who'd encountered his dark side, recognized Way-Way, too, and they'd cross the street to avoid him. At a run.

Sam had watched Way-Way's Progress, the Adventures of the Incredible Growing Man, from the time he was a boy. He and Way-Way were classmates, neighbors. They were always friendly, if never exactly friends. Sam was a stealthy, smirking kid, hanging around the fringes of school activities, watching for an opportunity to play his practical jokes—putting roadkill in people's lockers or setting off stink bombs in chemistry class. Way-Way, on the other hand, was Mr. Most Popular Stud, the big man on campus. Sam never minded standing in Way-Way's shadow—a man that size, it's hard not to.

One Friday night, in their junior year, their lives were welded together in a flash. It was a big night for both of them. Way-Way was walking home from a post-game victory party, a little beer-woozy and sexually spent, the conquering hero. Sam was driving his first stolen car. It was a beauty. A late-1950s Cadillac. Huge engine, sounded like a C-130. Seats like plush living room furniture. A trunk as wide as a house, bracketed by triple fins and torpedo taillights.

Sam spotted Way-Way staggering along the dark sidewalk, and he couldn't resist showing off. He pulled over, offered Way-Way a ride. They cruised the streets of their neighborhood, an all-night blues show on the radio, Muddy Waters spilling out the windows of the Great American Land Shark. Together, really together the first time in their parallel lives, Sam and Way-Way discovered the "joy" in joy-riding.

Then some asshole in a pickup truck blew through a stop sign and smashed the rear quarter-panel of the Cadillac. Spun the Caddy halfway around in the intersection, knocked Sam and Way-Way senseless. The other driver stumbled toward the car, blood all over his face.

"Get out of here," Sam said through clenched teeth.

"What?" Way-Way shook his head, clearing the cobwebs.

"Get the hell out of here, man. The car's not mine. They'll kick you off the team if they catch you."

Sam lurched out from behind the wheel and hugged the other driver, spinning him around, asking him questions, keeping his attention as a siren sounded nearby. Way-Way slipped away into the darkness.

The cops leaned on Sam, but he never talked. His silence meant a full year at the "boys' school," when he could've cut a better deal. But Way-Way couldn't afford the headlines. An arrest would've ruined the football hero's career. Way-Way went on to college and glory days, and he never forgot.

Since then, Sam gets into any kind of trouble, ever, and all he has to do is call Way-Way, who'd drop whatever he was doing to help. Nice to have that kind of safety net.

Sam turned as the man himself lumbered into the room. Way-Way wore a short-sleeved black sweatshirt and blue jeans. Big white Nikes on his feet. Fingerless black weightlifter's gloves on his hands. The tight sleeves of the shirt showed off his bulging arms. His face already was twisted into a determined scowl. He looked like he ought to be clinging to the side of a skyscraper somewhere, swatting at biplanes.

"You trying to scare me?"

"Just getting mentally prepared. Let's go scare *them*."

12

Ernesto Morelos bid farewell to his lunch *amigos* at the Barelas Coffee House, then busied himself with a toothpick while he drove back to work. Ernesto had gaps between his teeth, a white picket-fence of a mouth. A big meal left him with lots of dental hygiene to perform.

Lively *ranchera* music spilled from his radio as he cruised down South Broadway, past the *bodegas* and the burger joints, the rib shacks, and the radiator shops. The avenue was crowded with slow-moving cars, and Ernesto Morelos ran the numbers in his head as his gaze wandered among them. That Ford would net five grand in Juarez. This Chevy maybe six. Toyota pickups, four-wheel drive SUVs, worth twice that to some rancher in Chihuahua. He looked them over carefully for rust and tire wear and dings, sizing each one up. Ernesto approached a traffic jam with the same sensory thrill other people get at a produce stand.

Farther south, the traffic thinned to nothing and the character of the street changed. It was a highway now, speed limit fifty-five, wide shoulders sprinkled with broken glass. Set back from the road, among sandy acres littered with windblown trash, were warehouses and manufacturing plants and the giant white storage tanks of oil-and-gas jobbers. A pallet factory. An ancient brick power plant with shattered windows and its own flock of indoor pigeons. South of the city limits, Ernesto reached the land of the glittering junkyards. Salvage garages. Car crushers. Metal recyclers. Jim's Auto Parts and A-1 Auto Salvage and Manuel's Wrecking Service and Hub Cap City. And there, the last one, standing off by itself, Morelos Automotive—Sales and Service.

Not an imposing building, except for its color, which was taxicab yellow with Ernesto's name written large in black paint across the front. Three work bays, a small office. An acre of cars out back, surrounded by a six-foot privacy fence made of steel posts and roofing tin, topped by a shiny coil of razor wire. The fence required by the county because junkyards are eyesores, but to Ernesto the dusty wrecks packed tightly into the yard were things of beauty. The fence was also perfect for his main use—hiding hot cars until they could be shipped to Mexico.

He had another shipment ready to go, if the *chingada* paint would dry on that one truck. Nine vehicles, three to a tow rig, leaving tonight, ripping through the darkness to Ciudad Juarez. Each vehicle with fresh paint and paperwork. Everything legit, as long as no one looked too closely. And Ernesto kept enough palms greased at the border that nobody would look very hard.

He wheeled his Lincoln Continental into the gravel lot and parked in the reserved space outside his office. The work bay doors were closed against the cold, but the office windows glowed and he could see Moe moving around in there among the cluttered desks.

Moe was Ernesto's assistant, must be eighty years old now, a master at faking Motor Vehicle Division documentation. Moe was a papery wisp of a man who had to wear suspenders because he didn't have enough *panza* to cinch a belt around.

Ernesto should have such problems. He looked down at his ample gut and gave it a pat with his stubby hand. Jiggle. He snorted and looked in the mirror, gave his teeth a final check. All clear. He checked for redness in his brown eyes—he'd had a few beers at lunch—and made sure his thinning black hair was slicked across his bald spot. Satisfied, he finally turned off the purring car and opened the door.

An icy breeze sliced across the parking lot, and the sudden discomfort made him step lively in his cowboy boots to get into his warm office.

A bell on the glass door jangled as Ernesto puffed inside. Moe turned to look, and Ernesto saw he was wearing a green eyeshade, like a bookie in an old movie.

"What's with the visor?"

"Gotta shade my eyes," Moe said. "These fluorescent lights are killing me."

"Nothing wrong with these lights. They're bright. Good for reading."

"I tell you, I'm going blind." The old man was always short of breath. Everything he said sounded like a wheeze.

"Go to a doctor. But don't wear that stupid eyeshade around here. Makes the place look like a clip joint."

Moe grumbled and pulled the eyeshade off his head, which made his white hair stand out over his ears.

"Now you look like Bozo," Ernesto said.

"Leave me alone." Moe turned his back on him and sorted through some papers, sounded like he said "prick" under his breath. Ernesto managed to keep from laughing.

He peered through the window set into the upper half of the heavy door that connected to the garage. Chuco perched on a stack of tires in there, flapping his lips while the painters and body men peeled the last of the masking tape off a truck destined for tonight's shipment. Chuco, Ernesto's nephew, with his bandana around his head and his tattoos and his gold jewelry. Mr. Gangbanger. Always a gun hidden away somewhere in his baggy jeans. Like owning a *pistola* meant you never had to do any work. The kid was no damned good, even if he was Maria's son. No ambition. Big attitude. Reckless. Dangerous.

Perfect, really, for Uncle Ernesto's needs. A cash business like his has its hazards. Some *pendejo* might think he could rob Ernesto, take advantage. Or some dissatisfied customer might come storming in, want to give Ernesto a thrashing. It happens. Better to have somebody like Chuco around, just in case. At least none of his hot-headed friends were with him today.

Ernesto pressed his palm against the glass, felt the cold seep through from the unheated garage. Brrr. He turned away.

The phone rang, and Moe answered it as Ernesto plopped down behind his elbow-worn desk and began to unwrap a fresh cigar.

Moe said, "Yeah, he's here. *Momentito—*"

The old man looked quizzically at the receiver in his hand. "They hung up."

"They'll call back. You get all those titles notarized?"

"Each one with a different date."

Ernesto ran the cigar under his nose, inhaling deeply.

"Registrations up to date?"

"It's all done, I tell you."

"All right, what about—"

The doorbell jingled and Ernesto swiveled in his chair to greet the customer, tell 'em to shut the door before all the cold wind gets inside. But the wind stopped as a giant ducked through the door. His shoulders and chest filled the doorway, blocking the wind, practically blocking all light from entering.

"The fuck?" Ernesto dropped his unlit cigar on the floor.

The giant had a shaved head and a big mustache, and he looked like a circus strongman in a cartoon, the kind who wow audiences by bending railroad spikes and lifting barbells that resemble big black balloons. He stepped to one side, and Sam Hill followed him into the office.

Ernesto got a sudden rumble in his full belly. He knew what Sam Hill wanted, and Sam apparently had gone out and hired himself Godzilla to make sure he got it.

The big man stepped in front of the connecting door, blocking the window. No help coming from the garage. Moe was no good. He clutched his scrawny chest and fell into the nearest chair.

"Ernesto. Old buddy. How you doing?"

Sam Hill giving him the hundred-watt smile, coming over, cocking a leg to sit on the corner of Ernesto's desk. Bastard, always acting like he's better than the rest of us. A *specialist*.

"Doing okay, Sam." Ernesto shrugged his shoulders, but kept his hands in plain sight. "Business could be better, you know, but what can you do?"

"That's why I came by. Wanted to thank you for sending some business my way."

"You mean that Thunderbird? Where is it anyway?"

"Ran into a little hitch." Sam Hill smiled at him. It was not a happy smile, and it gave Ernesto a chill. "It's going to take another day or two to deliver."

"Oh, that's okay," Ernesto said quickly. "Couple more days. I'll just let the customer know—"

"Why don't I save us all some time and deliver the car myself. Take it straight to the client."

Ernesto let the smile slide off his face.

"That's no good, Sam. The customer, he wants me to paint it."

"It's got brand-new paint now."

"He wants a different color. And there's the paperwork—"

"Maybe I'll just call the client." Sam's blue eyes glittered. "See how he wants to play it."

"Let me call him—"

"What's wrong, Ernesto? You act like you don't want to tell me about the client. Who's this guy, Batman? He's got a secret identity?"

Ernesto tried to laugh, but his throat was dry. "No, nothing like that."

"Tell me the customer's name."

Ernesto glanced over at the behemoth blocking the door and tried to swallow. The man crossed his arms over his chest. Two sides of beef. He glared at Ernesto from beneath heavy black eyebrows.

Better to look at Sam, who still rested nonchalantly on the corner of his desk.

"I don't know, Sam. It's confidential—"

"I'm in kind of a hurry here, buddy. Got to feed Way-Way before he gets cranky."

Ernesto glanced at the giant. Way-Way. He knew that name, knew the man's reputation. A sharp pain stabbed Ernesto in the bowels, made him regret his spicy lunch. He wiped his forehead and his hand came away wet with beer sweat.

"Okay," he said. "Just let me think a second."

Ernesto knew the client's name. If that was all Sam wanted, why not give it to him? Maybe he'd leave and take that fucking hulk with him. But the client, Phil Ortiz, was more dangerous than either of these two goons. They might give Ernesto a whipping, but they weren't likely to kill him. Ortiz? Word was: Make him the least bit unhappy, and your corpse gets dumped out in the desert somewhere. Vulture lunch.

Ernesto sighed and shook his head. "Sorry, Sam. I promised I wouldn't say."

"I don't like that answer." Sam rocked to his feet and stood too close, crowding Ernesto, scowling down at him.

The front door jangled open and a blast of cold wind chilled Ernesto. Heads swiveled as everyone turned to look.

Chuco stood there, one hand holding the door open, the other loose by his side. The bandana rode low over his ebony eyes. At the sight of him, Ernesto felt a small speed bump of hope inside his chest.

"Everything okay in here, *tio*?"

"Come in, Chuco. Just discussing a little business with these men."

Chuco came into the office and let the door swing closed. He sidestepped to his left, keeping his distance from the giant *gringo*. Next to the big man, the bantamweight Chuco seemed tiny. With his loose flannel shirt buttoned to the chin and his baggy pants, he looked like a kid dressed up in his daddy's clothes. But Ernesto relaxed a little. Some rattlesnakes are tiny, too.

The big man raised his chin at Chuco. "*Private* business," he said in a voice like distant thunder.

"Chill, homey," Chuco said. He spread his feet a little, threw out his skinny chest. "My uncle's got no secrets from me. We're *familia*."

"That right, Ernesto?" Sam said. "The kid here knows all your secrets? Maybe we ought to ask *him* the client's name."

Ernesto shifted uncomfortably in his chair. "He doesn't know. I wouldn't mix him up in something like that."

"Like *what*, Ernesto?" Sam Hill leaned over him. Ernesto couldn't rock back any farther in his chair without tipping over.

"Just a simple boost, right?" Sam said. "No big deal. Chuco's so pure, he can't hear about that?"

"Hey!" Chuco snarled. "You got something to say to me, you look me in the eye."

The giant rocked forward, took a step away from the door. Chuco danced backward a couple of steps.

"I don't know what's goin' down here," Chuco said. "But you boys gonna leave now."

He grasped the tails of his flannel shirt and pulled them up to his chest, exposing the black grip of a pistol tucked into the waistband of his jeans.

Sam and Way-Way exchanged a look, then Sam turned back to Ernesto.

"This the way you want to play it? Let your nephew threaten people with guns?"

Ernesto shrugged, trying to keep a smile off his face.

"Sorry, Sam. But I told you. I've got nothing to say. There's no sense yelling about it. Chuco's right. This meeting's over."

Sam considered this answer, looking from one man to the other. When his eyes lit on his partner, he raised his eyebrows. The giant tilted his shaved head to one side, pointed at his own chest with his thumb. Sam gave his own head the tiniest shake and cut his eyes toward the parking lot.

"You two *pendejos* make up your minds yet?" Chuco said. "You look like you're deciding to steal third base."

Sam's mouth turned up at the corners. "No, we're sending gang signals. You know all about those, don't you?"

Sam waved his hands around, forming nonsense letters in the air. Hunched his shoulders over, let his arms dangle like an ape's, mimicking the shrugging street-corner dance of the homeboy. He finished with one hand upraised, giving Chuco the finger.

Chuco's face hardened, and his lips pressed thin. His hand went to the pistol at his waist. "You want a taste of this?"

"No, we're leaving," Sam said. "I have other ways of getting information. Without a lot of cheap gunfighter theatrics."

The light dimmed in Chuco's eyes while he tried to decipher what that meant. Sam went out the jangling door, and the giant squeaked through behind him. They walked with their heads lowered into the wind and got into Sam's Chevy.

"I saw that big *gringo* block the door, *tio*," Chuco said. "I went out the back and came around. Good thing, huh?"

"Yes." Ernesto took a deep breath and blew it out. "A good thing."

13

INSIDE THE CHEVY, Sam started the car and sat blowing on his hands. Way-Way filled the seat next to him and he didn't act cold, even with the short sleeves. He peered through the office windows, where Chuco had turned his back to them, his hands dancing as he spoke. Ernesto leaned over in his chair to see around Chuco, keeping a wary eye on the Chevy.

"That went well," Way-Way grumbled.

"Yeah."

"I liked the part where you did the chicken dance."

"Thanks. It's a gift."

Way-Way glanced over at him, then stared back out the windshield at Morelos Automotive.

"What you want to do now?"

Sam cleared his throat. "Drive away."

"You think Ernesto doesn't know the client's name. Or he would've given it up."

"No, he knows it," Sam said. "I think old Ernesto missed his true calling. He should've been an actor."

"A liar, you mean."

"A character actor. Sweaty, sleazy type, the kind who play gangsters and bagmen and rats."

"Dirtbags."

"Right. Ernesto looks like all those guys. He could be a big star."

Way-Way squinted. "He looks like Ernest Borgnine."

"Yeah, somebody like that."

"I liked 'McHale's Navy.'"

"You're getting off track here."

"Right. We just gonna sit here or what?"

Sam put the car into gear.

"We're leaving," he said. "For a minute."

His tires threw up dust as he gunned the car out of the gravel lot and bumped up onto South Broadway.

"Where we going?" Way-Way asked.

"Got to get something out of the trunk."

Sam pulled off the road after a mile and parked behind a transmission shop.

"Wait here." Sam popped open his door and went around to the back of the car. He checked the empty parking lot, then opened the trunk. He was bending over, reaching for a steel toolbox, when Way-Way appeared at his elbow.

"You should wait in the car."

"I like fresh air."

"It's freezing. And you're too obvious. You stop traffic, standing around."

"I like to feel the wind in my hair."

"You don't have any—"

"Fresh air's good for muscle development."

"Jesus, you're a fucking mutant, you know that?"

Sam opened the toolbox and lifted out the upper tray full of screwdrivers and wrenches and pliers. Underneath were more tools and a bundle wrapped in an orange shop towel. Sam picked it up, removed the rag and showed Way-Way the .38-caliber Smith & Wesson revolver he'd hidden there.

"Thought we might want this," he said.

"Why didn't you take it with you in the first place?"

"I figured Ernesto would cave so quickly, we wouldn't need a piece."

Way-Way gave him a look. "You *forgot* it, didn't you?"

"Get in the car," Sam said. "You drive."

Way-Way turned the Chevy around and eased it forward, peeking around the transmission shop. When the road was clear in both directions, he rocked the car up onto the blacktop and floored it.

"Chuco's gun was a semi-automatic," Sam yelled over the roaring engine. "He had it stuck in his pants. Anybody carries a gun there—even someone stupid as Chuco—he's gonna have the safety on so he doesn't shoot off his own dick."

"I don't know," Way-Way said. "That kid seemed extra stupid."

"Trust me. He goes for that gun, and I'll shoot him before he can thumb off the safety."

Way-Way barely let up on the gas as the Chevy rocketed off the pavement onto Ernesto's rutted gravel lot. The car shuddered to a stop in a cloud of dust, right outside the office door. Sam was out of the Chevy before it finished rocking.

Through the windows, he could see Chuco sitting in a chair, his feet up on his uncle's desk. Ernesto still sat behind his desk where they'd left him, and his eyes went wide as Sam bounded through the door.

Sam pointed his pistol at Chuco's head as the youngster jerked and tried to get up. Chuco's hands went involuntarily toward the gun in his belt, but he hesitated and it was too late. He froze in place and his eyes narrowed.

Sam felt Way-Way's immense presence behind him, and said, "Watch the doors. I got these fuckers cold."

Sam stepped over to Chuco, pressed the revolver's barrel against the kid's forehead.

"The gun."

Chuco slowly snaked a hand under his clothes and came up with the little semi-automatic. Sam took it from his hand, and stepped back.

Ernesto hadn't moved a muscle. The white-haired old man still sat in the back, clutching his chest. He didn't look so good.

Sam clicked off the safety on the kid's pistol and took another step back, so he could keep Chuco and Ernesto covered with the two guns. Way-Way was at the connecting door, peering into the work bays.

"Those mechanics look curious," he said mildly. "They're coming this way."

"I don't want them in here," Sam said.

"You got it."

Sam focused his attention on Ernesto. The fat man was sweating, and he couldn't seem to take his eyes off the pistols.

"Morelos!"

Ernesto's head snapped up and he blinked.

"Doesn't have to be this way," Sam said. "Just tell me the client's name and we'll clear out of here. Nobody'll get hurt."

Two swarthy mechanics in filthy gray coveralls pushed open the connecting door. The one in the front carried a short-handled sledgehammer.

Way-Way casually threw an uppercut into the guy's chest. Sounded like a fastball hitting a mitt, followed by the distinct crackle of broken ribs. The mechanic flew backward, and the back of his skull crashed into the second guy's face. They went down in a spray of blood. Way-Way closed the door and stepped to one side.

Sam sighed. "Okay, a few people will get hurt. Especially anybody else who tries to come through that door. But I don't want to shoot you, Ernesto. We're businessmen. We shouldn't be acting like this."

Ernesto had a look of deep sadness and revulsion on his face, as if he'd shit his pants. Sam considered that a definite possibility. Little something in the air.

Chuco muttered, but Sam didn't even turn to look at him. He just thumbed back the hammer on the revolver pointed at Chuco's head. The kid sat still.

"If I tell you," Ernesto said, "I'm a dead man."

"No, you got it backward. You *don't* tell me, you're dead right now. You keep stalling, and I'll make it slow."

Ernesto gulped.

"Shoot you in the ear," Sam said, aiming the punk's little pistol.

Ernesto shook his head.

"Shoot you in the hand. You'll never jerk off again."

"Sam, it's just not possible. Too much could go wrong."

"Look around, Ernesto. Things are already wrong."

Ernesto clamped his wide mouth shut, breathed heavily through his nose.

"You want me to shoot your nephew?" Sam said. "Nothing would make me happier than to erase this little fuck off the face of the Earth. You gonna tell me before or after I shoot him?"

Sam guessed right. The tactic got Ernesto talking.

"Don't shoot the boy," he said. "My sister—"

"He's a worthless punk."

"True, but—"

"*Tio!*"

"Be still." Sam waved the revolver at the kid until he obeyed. "But what, Ernesto?"

"He's my sister's kid. You kill him, I'll never hear the end of it. Maria's one of those women—"

"I know the type."

"Please don't shoot him. Shoot me, but don't shoot Chuco."

Sam pretended to think it over. Ernesto's eyes got even wider while he waited, staring at the guns. He looked like a freaking goldfish.

"Tell me the name, Ernesto."

Another mechanic appeared in the window by Way-Way. The guy cautiously pushed open the door a few inches, peering inside. Way-Way slammed his arm against the steel door, which smacked the man off his feet as it banged shut.

"All right!" Ernesto shouted. "I'll tell you. Then you get out of here and leave me alone. I've got a shipment going out tonight. I can't have the cops coming around."

"Tell me the name." Sam's arms were getting tired, holding up the pistols.

"Just don't shoot nobody, all right? I'll tell you and you leave."

"Tell me now."

"It's Phil Ortiz."

Sam absorbed the name and ran it through his mental files. "Who?"

"Phil Ortiz. You don't know him?"

"Never heard of him."

"He asked for you by name," Ernesto said. "Told me to get you to steal the T-Bird. Happy now? It's Phil Ortiz. And you don't even know who I'm talking about."

"Who is he?"

"Big drug dealer in the South Valley, worth millions. Collects low-riders. You don't know him?"

Ernesto's mouth spread wide, and he looked as if he was trying not to laugh.

"I think you're lying," Sam said.

"It's the truth! Phil Ortiz. He had the keys, told me when and where. I didn't know there was anything wrong with the boost until you come walking in here."

"See, there you go again. I never said there was anything wrong with the boost. I said delivery was delayed. You know more than you're saying, Ernesto."

"I told you the name. I swear, on my life, that's all I know."

Sam glanced over at Way-Way, who stood with his head bent forward so he could see through the window into the garage.

"There's a phone in there," he said, "and one of those little pricks is calling the cops."

"Stop him!" Ernesto cried. "I don't want cops sniffing around. Not today."

"You stop him," Sam said. "We're out of here."

He backed up, keeping the pistols pointed their way. He paused to let Way-Way go behind him, out into the cold, then ran for the Chevy.

14

SAM STEERED THE CHEVY onto I-25, headed north, and drove a couple of miles before Way-Way finally spoke.

"Ortiz is a drug dealer?"

"That's what the man said."

"I hate drug dealers."

"I know you do."

Way-Way put one fist inside the other and cracked his knuckles. Sounded like small-arms fire.

"We going to see him now?" he asked.

"No."

"Why not?"

"Because we still don't know what's going on here. We don't know this guy."

"We know he put that junkie in your trunk."

"Yes, but why me?"

Way-Way grunted. "We go see him and find out."

"It's no good. We need to be prepared."

"You got me and two pistols. What more do you need?"

"Information. I have to know *why* before I know what to do next."

"We'll get the information from him."

"You just want to fight some more. Those mechanics didn't give you anything."

Way-Way flexed his arms in front of him. Sam felt like the car was filling with airbags.

"I'm pumped," Way-Way said. "Perfect time to go visit this Ortiz."

"No. Ernesto's probably on the phone right now, warning him that we're coming. Let him worry."

Sam got off the freeway at Lead Avenue and steered toward downtown. Way-Way asked, "Where we going?"

"Taking you home."

"We're done?"

"For now. I'll call you later, once I get this shit figured out. I need to talk to Robin. Get her on the computer. See what we can find on Mr. Phil Ortiz. You're at the bar tonight, right?"

"Yeah. Call if you need me."

"You can just walk off the job anytime you want?"

"Sure."

"What about the owner? What's-his-name. Hutchins. He doesn't mind?"

"He gives me any static and I look at him like this."

Sam glanced over to see Way-Way doing the full-bore bar-bouncer glare.

"That scares the shit out of him."

"Pretty much."

"I'm not surprised."

Way-Way's face relaxed and he shook out his shoulders. "Stan keeps on more bouncers than he needs anyway. Who gets rowdy at The Tropics? Two guys like me can keep watch over the whole place."

"There are *other* guys like you?"

Way-Way flashed a smile, his teeth like bright eggs in his bird's nest of a mustache.

"A few."

15

WHEN THE PHONE CALL CAME, Phil Ortiz was in the garage behind his South Valley home, buffing the rounded fenders of a '49 Buick Super just back from the restoration garage. The broad-shouldered car was a work of art—shiny black with red and yellow flames creeping up the hood, a dazzling chrome grille like a Louis Armstrong grin. Chopped and channeled, its split windshield reduced to a narrow pillbox slit. He'd had the Buick lowered onto thirteen-inch wheels, barely two inches of clearance between the frame and the concrete floor.

"This one," Phil shouted over the ringing phone, "will bring home the trophies!"

Johnny Murdoch, Phil's enforcer, said nothing as he hiked to the phone on the far wall. The brick garage was four thousand square feet, climate-controlled, bigger and cleaner than most people's homes. Two overhead doors on one side, theft-alarmed windows set into each end to allow light inside. A glass case full of trophies along one wall, next to a washing-up sink and a pegboard holding the keys to the fourteen cars parked in the garage. Low-riders and hot rods, restored to pristine condition, rarely driven. Phil regularly buffed the cars himself, keeping the dust at bay, admiring his reflection in the car's paint—always a dozen coats, thick and glossy as lipstick.

The cars were worth nearly a million dollars. An expensive hobby, but one that kept Phil happy, one that made all the risks worthwhile. He could live off his legitimate businesses and be a wealthy man by most standards. But he kept wholesaling the drugs, kept amassing his riches, so he could indulge his good taste in all things, including cars. Whenever Phil Ortiz saw anything he wanted—this Buick, a new wardrobe, an expensive woman—he always could afford it.

He couldn't hear what Johnny Murdoch was muttering into the phone, but he saw him shake his head. Murdoch, his face set on permanent glower, denying someone access. The harsh sunlight pouring through the windows glinted on his Brylcreemed red-brown hair and illuminated the ancient acne scars on his cheeks, looked like the surface of the moon. Murdoch was in his mid-thirties, five years younger than Phil, but he looked ten years older. His nose was flat and his brows were heavy with scar tissue. With his broad, sloping shoulders and his V-shaped torso under the gray sweatshirt, Murdoch looked like exactly what he was—a former middleweight boxer. Murderin' Murdoch they'd called him, back when he still ducked into the ring to go toe-to-toe with hot young properties the promoters were grooming for championships. He'd probably still be there, taking tiny purses in exchange for punishment, if Phil hadn't made him a better offer. In the three years since, Murdoch had proven worthy of his nickname, several times over.

Phil sometimes wondered, though, whether he'd made a mistake, putting so much trust in a man who'd spent a lifetime taking shots to the head. Murdoch was fine when following orders. He never questioned, never objected to anything Phil asked him to do. But when he tried to exercise his own initiative, Murdoch invariably fucked up.

Look at this current situation. Phil had a plan for Sam Hill, a way to get even for past sins. Commission him to steal a car, then call the cops, put them on the thief's trail. What better way to punish Hill? Poetic justice, they called it. Phil always liked that term.

But Murdoch had to get creative. He'd been told to make sure Hill wouldn't have any trouble stealing the T-Bird from that asshole Blankenship. Unfortunately, he discovered Armas was a snitch while the two of them were at the lawyer's house. He hadn't consulted Phil first. Just popped Tony Armas, right between the eyes. Which would've been fine by Phil. That's the way he would've handled the rat himself.

It was Murdoch's next move—putting Armas' corpse in the T-Bird's trunk—that raised the problem. Given a dead snitch, Phil would've disposed of the body in a way that couldn't be traced back to him. But Murdoch, that punchy bastard, had hidden the body in the car Hill was coming to steal. Thought it was a clever move, raising the stakes when the cops caught Hill, but Phil knew it was stupid. If the cops found the body, they'd trace Armas back to Phil Ortiz. They'd come asking their questions. Once again, Phil would be left to clean up after his enforcer.

When Murdoch told him about Armas—*after* Phil tipped Lieutenant Stanton, after it was too late to call the whole thing off—Phil had felt like killing the muscle-bound moron. But, so far, he hadn't heard anything from the police. Somehow, Sam Hill avoided the dragnet Phil set into motion. But Armas' corpse still floated around out there somewhere, and it worried Phil.

Murdoch cupped the phone. "It's that guy Morelos."

"Not now."

"He says it's an emergency."

Phil left his rag on the Buick's fender and crossed the room, thinking: The hell's wrong with Morelos? You do business with idiots ...

"Ernesto?"

"Phil. Glad I found you. We got problems."

Morelos paused to catch his breath. Phil pictured him as he'd last seen him, behind his desk at his claptrap garage, big shit-eating grin on his face. He didn't sound so happy now.

"That guy we talked about? That thief. You know who I mean."

"Yes. Be careful what you say."

"Right." Ernesto gulped into the phone and continued. "He came by here a while ago with this guy, looked like a fucking ox—"

"What did he want?"

"Your name."

Phil said nothing for a moment. Sam Hill was quicker than he'd expected.

"Did you tell him?"

"I had to, Phil. I'm sorry. But he had guns and—"

"Shut up. You say too much."

"Sorry. I'm upset. I think Moe's dead."

"Moe?"

"Old guy worked in my office? Handled all my paperwork? They scared him into a heart attack or something. He's not breathin.'"

"Did you call an ambulance?"

"Yeah."

"Before you called me?"

"Well, he's dying—"

Phil cleared his throat to cut Ernesto off. "When you deal with me, you put my business first."

"I'm *sorry*. Nothing I could do. Let me make it up to you—"

"The thief and his friend. Are they on the way here?"

"Maybe. That's why I called."

Phil could hear a siren whooping in the background.

"The ambulance is here. I gotta go. I can't let 'em call the cops. I've got a shipment going out tonight—"

Phil hung up the phone. He stroked his close-cropped beard, absorbing the news, then turned to find Johnny Murdoch watching him, the man's face a pitted wooden mask.

"We may be having company," Phil said. "Let's go in the house, call the boys."

Murdoch stepped out the garage door first and checked the surrounding pastures and country lanes for any sign of trouble. Phil followed him out, turned on the garage alarm, and locked it up.

They hurried along a sidewalk to the back door of Phil's house, a Tudor fortress made of the same mottled gray brick as the garage. Once inside, Phil locked that door, too.

Murdoch went to the living room and checked each window before closing the curtains. The ex-boxer had a pistol in his hand.

"That guy Sam Hill knows my name," Phil said. "He showed up at Ernesto's place, showed some guns, and Ernesto told him."

Murdoch cut his eyes to the east, in the direction of Morelos' shop.

"We'll deal with him later," Phil said. "For now, I want to be ready in case Hill comes here."

Murdoch nodded. "I'll make some calls."

Phil went into his home office, which was next to the living room, with windows that overlooked the front yard. He peered out from behind the curtains. Nobody out there in the slanted afternoon sunshine. Nothing to see but a couple of distant horses and Murodch's beat-up truck parked in the front driveway.

Goddamn you, Sam Hill. You should be in the hands of the cops by now, thanks to my well-placed phone tip. Instead, you're running around town, asking questions, sweating Morelos. And I'm watching for you out my windows, acting like a worried old woman.

Phil crossed the room and sat in the leather chair behind his mahogany desk. He opened a drawer, pulled out a Beretta and popped the slide. He set the pistol on his desk, then tried to relax.

He had nothing to fear. Sam Hill was a fucking mutt. He didn't have the *cojones* to face down Phil Ortiz, no matter how many pet gorillas he had on the leash.

Hill and his bodyguard want to see me, he thought, they'd better phone first. Because if they come to my home to make trouble, I won't waste time talking.

Phil felt a smile tighten his face. The showdown might be swift, but he hoped not. He wanted some time to work on Sam Hill, teach him a few things before he dies. Like respect for another man's property.

16

ROBIN MITCHELL WAS DOWN on her knees in the corner, her butt in the air, when Sam walked into her office at Mitch's Auto Salvage later Tuesday afternoon.

"Lose something?"

She peered into the narrow gap between a file cabinet and the wall and jabbed into the dark space with a long screwdriver. "Those idiot cops knocked over a coffee cup when they were searching the place."

"A screwdriver would seem to be the wrong tool for a spill," he said.

"The cup was full of hex nuts. I'm spearing them with this screwdriver."

She turned her head to look up at him. Her glossy black ponytail brushed the floor.

"You could move the file cabinet for me," she said.

"I've got a bad back."

She smiled as she got to her feet. "I knew you'd say that."

Robin brushed at the knees of her jeans, then straightened up, and looked around the office.

"The cops wrecked the place," she said. "My crew's been cleaning up all day."

"You must be about done, if you're down on the floor, spearing nuts."

"I think of it as therapy."

"Ouch."

Robin fell into her swivel chair and put her steel-toed boots up on her paper-strewn desk. She rested her hands on her silver belt buckle and intertwined her fingers.

"You want to tell me what you've been up to?"

Sam needed her help, and she'd know if he lied. She always knew. So he told her the whole story—the corpse and the cops and Billy and Chuco and Phil Ortiz. He tried to make the violence at Ernesto's sound more comical than it had felt at the time.

She listened without expression. When he was done, she said, "So this is why my shop got wrecked. Because you're running around town, playing bad boy."

"It wasn't my fault—"

"You've always been a troublemaker, Sam. A pain in the ass."

"I prefer to think of myself as fun-loving."

She arched an eyebrow. "You don't know fun until you've got a backache from sorting chrome bumpers by model and year."

"Took all day, huh?"

"Stanton encourages his men to be sloppy."

Sam leaned against the file cabinet and crossed his arms over his chest. He looked down at his feet, then back up at her, gave her a big smile.

"Uh-oh," she said.

"What?"

"That look. It's the Gomer."

Caught. He'd forgotten he ever told her about the Gomer.

"I don't know what you mean." He played it straight, but he was fighting back laughter.

"That's the Gomer, the con man's special," she said. "Your old man taught it to you. Kind of a hick grin, an 'aw shucks' shrug, supposed to warm people up. Then you hit them up for something."

He let the laughter loose. "Okay, you got me. Sometimes, I fall back on the tried-and-true. I do need something."

Robin gave him a level look. "What's in it for me?"

"You always get right to the point."

"I've lost a whole day's work around here. And my nuts are stuck behind the file cabinet."

Sam grinned. "Mine appear to be in a vise. Tell you what. Soon as this is over, I'll give you that Thunderbird."

"The one with the dead guy?"

"I'll take the dead guy out first."

"That car's red hot. I wouldn't drive it around the block. And it probably smells bad."

"Clean it up and sell it. Look real nice in a midnight blue."

Robin tilted her head to one side, considering it. "What is it that you need?"

"Info on this guy Phil Ortiz. I never heard of him."

"You must've run across him somewhere. Why else would he set you up?"

"That's what I need to find out. Could you get on your computer and see what you can turn up on him? Check all the usual places—Internet, newspapers, credit reports, Motor Vehicle—"

"I know what 'the usual places' means."

Sam felt himself flush. "I don't want to go up against Ortiz until I know more about him."

Robin dropped her feet to the floor and leaned toward him. A strand of loose hair clung to her cheek. Sam wanted to touch it.

She said, "Why go after him at all?"

"I let him set me up and do nothing?"

"He set you up for a reason."

"Right. I need to know what that reason is."

"Maybe he's taunting you. Maybe he *wants* you to come after him."

"You think?"

"Maybe he's following you around, waiting for you to go back to wherever you stashed that T-Bird."

"I've been watching. Nobody's tailed me since the cops picked up Billy."

Robin wrapped her hand around her left wrist and squeezed until it popped loudly. She'd broken that wrist roller-skating when she was fourteen; Sam remembered her at Mitch's shop, grease and grime all over the white plaster cast. Her wrist had made that cracking noise ever since. Always set his teeth on edge.

"Listen to yourself, Sam. Watching for tails. Waving guns around. Wouldn't it be better to just sit quietly for a few days? At least until Lieutenant Stanton settles down."

"I'm not worried about Stanton. This other guy, Ortiz, worries me."

She sighed and turned toward her desk. "I'll boot up the computer and run him through."

She hit some buttons on the computer as she spoke, and the machine bloop-blooped through a phone number.

"You going to hang around while I do this?"

"Nothing I'd love more, ma'am, but I've got errands to run."

"More gun-waving?"

Sam boosted himself away from the file cabinet and moved closer to her. "Need to go check on Billy, see if my lawyer's sprung him yet. Run by the house, get something to eat."

He reached out, caught the strand of hair between his fingers, and tucked it behind her warm ear. She smiled up at him, and the air got thinner in the room, made it hard to breathe. Then she caught herself and looked toward the computer, and the moment was gone.

Sam turned around, grasped the heavy file cabinet, and walked it a few inches from the wall. "There you go. Your nuts have been freed."

"I feel better already," she said, but her eyes never left the computer screen.

He went out the door, leaving her in the grasp of the Web.

17

SAM WAS CLIMBING INTO the still-warm Caprice when his phone rang.

"Hello?"

"Hi, Sam."

"Hello, *William*. Are you a free man?"

"Your lawyer made 'em turn me loose."

"Bail?"

"No charges. Just questioned me for hours."

"About me?"

"Mostly."

"And what did you say?"

"Nothing, Sam. You know that."

"Good boy. They ask about Armas?"

"Yeah. And some guy named Ortiz. You ever hear of him?"

"His name's come up."

"Who is he?"

"Not on the phone. I'll fill you in later. Where are you now?"

"Your lawyer gave me a lift to where I left my car. She's one tough broad, huh?"

"We grew up together. She used to beat me up on the playground."

"I believe it."

"And William?"

"Yeah?"

"Don't say 'broad.' It's rude."

"You hear it on TV all the time."

"That proves my point. TV's got no class."

"Right."

"Go home, William. Read a book. It's a good night for all of us to stay indoors."

"Okay, Sam, but one more thing: when they were questioning me, a guy in a suit brought Stanton some paperwork. Said something about a search warrant."

"My place?"

"I couldn't see. But home might not be the safest place right now."

Sam thought it over. "No, I'm going home. I'm tired. I'm hungry. If Stanton's waiting, I'll deal with him."

"Okay. Call if you need me."

Sam tucked the phone in his pocket and slipped the Chevy into gear. He needed to get home in a hurry, in case Stanton was there, turning the place upside down.

He used the freeways to skirt the downtown high-rises, weaving through traffic, pushing the speed limits. Even with a quick stop at a Walgreens, he made it home inside twenty minutes.

Stanton was waiting by the front door, paperwork in hand. His partner, Delgado, stood next to him, looking tired and cold, his hands in the pockets of his overcoat. Two uniforms waited nearby, one of them smoking a cigarette, fogging the air in the courtyard.

Facing down this assemblage of authority was Joe Winter, his fists on his scrawny hips, his round belly thrust forward, his cheeks fiery red. The on-site manager of the condos, seventy-some years old, yelling at the cops and too deaf to hear their replies. With his thick glasses and his oversized dentures, Joe resembled an angry gopher.

As Sam climbed out of his car, Joe spotted him and came hurrying over. He wore a white sweatshirt with writing on the front, the letters stretched wide over his belly: "I RETIRED so I could stay home and see what the hell my wife DOES all day."

Joe made a big deal about being retired, but everyone knew he was worth a fortune. Not only did he manage the condos, but he owned a dozen automatic car washes all over town. Joe raked in a bundle from the car washes without ever getting out of his reclining chair.

"There you are, Sam," he puffed. "These cops want to search your place, but I told them that wasn't right, when you weren't even home. They tried to get me to open—"

"Nice shirt." Sam spoke loudly to make sure Joe could hear.

"What?" Joe looked down, read his own belly. "Oh, yeah. I like this one."

"What's the answer?"

"To what?"

"Your wife. What does she do all day?"

Joe scratched his grizzled head. "Mostly, she yells at me for lying around, doing nothing."

Sam laughed, but Joe still looked concerned.

"These cops—"

"Don't worry about them, Joe. I'll take care of it. Go get in out of the cold."

"You're sure it's all right?"

"Sure."

Joe turned away and nearly ran into Stanton, who was charging over with the search warrant. The old man dodged to the side and hurried away, muttering, "Fucking cops."

Stanton's eyebrows shot up his florid forehead, and he wheeled toward Joe, but Sam caught his arm.

"Want to see me, Lieutenant?"

"Did you hear—"

"I didn't hear anything."

Stanton ground his teeth together, working the muscles in his jaws. Then he said, "I've got a warrant to search your place."

"For what?"

"Here's your copy of the warrant. Read it for yourself."

Sam flipped the pages and pretended to scan the document. "Looks a little vague."

"Go to the last page, where it's signed by the judge. That's all you need to know."

Sam folded the warrant and tucked it inside his jacket. "Okay, what are we standing around here for?"

He glanced at the other condos as he led Stanton back to his front door. Neighbors were silhouetted in some of the windows, attracted by the hubbub. Embarrassed, Sam fumbled with his keys as he unlocked the door.

As Sam went inside, Stanton said, "Hey! Where do you think you're going?"

"Observing the search."

"Bullshit. You'll wait outside."

"No. I don't want you breaking my stuff. You can search all you want, but I'm watching."

"Nothing requires me to allow it," Stanton said.

"Do it my way, or I call my attorney and we fight the warrant in court."

Stanton winced. "Lorena Alvarado?"

"That's right. Maybe I'll call the TV stations, too."

The lieutenant's blue eyes bulged and he looked like he could chew a phone book in half. But he got himself under control and said, "Have it your way. Watch all you want, but don't touch anything. Stay out of our way or I'll cuff you and dump you out here in the yard."

"Fair enough." Sam reached in his jacket and pulled out a camera he'd bought at Walgreens, one of those disposable cardboard models, and held it up. "You won't mind if I take pictures."

"Are you kidding me?"

"Just to protect against breakage. I've got a big record collection. It's worth a lot of money."

"We don't care about your records."

"But I do. I'll take a few pictures. Make sure everything gets put back where it belongs."

Stanton grumbled, but finally agreed.

Sam stepped out of his way and said, "Have at it. There's a pistol in the bedside table. It's loaded, but hasn't been fired in months. Registration's in the same drawer."

Delgado hurried past to retrieve the gun.

Stanton gave Sam the hard eye. "What do you need with a gun?"

"Rats."

"What?"

"Extermination."

"You're telling me you've got *rats* here?"

"Just be careful, reaching under stuff."

The uniformed cops looked at each other, not sure whether to laugh or run. Stanton shucked his overcoat and started ordering people around.

Sam backed away and leaned against the living room wall, camera in hand.

He followed the cops from room to room as they searched through his life. They pawed through his clothes and handled his dishes and lifted up cushions and moved furniture. It was uncomfortable at first, but he tried to relax. He knew they'd find nothing incriminating. He kept his place completely clean.

The disposable camera came equipped with an electronic flash. Anytime Sam thought the cops were getting sloppy, he'd fire off a frame. The strobe would freeze everybody for a second, slow the cops down, remind them to be careful. Sam got to where he was almost enjoying himself.

His place wasn't that large and, with four cops working it, the search only took an hour. Stanton told the uniformed cops to beat it, and he and Delgado went to the living room for one last look around.

"Didn't find anything?" Sam said.

"You know we didn't," Stanton snarled. "You're too careful for that."

"I try to be a cautious man."

Stanton's lip curled and he turned away, began shrugging into his coat.

"What's with the search, Lieutenant? Why are you suddenly so interested in me?"

Stanton turned back, his face flushed. "I've *always* been interested in you, Hill. I've watched you for years, boosting cars and pulling your little scams. Mister Trickster. Think you're so damned smart."

Sam looked over at Delgado, who kept his head down, busy with his overcoat. Looked like he was trying not to laugh.

"I get it," Sam said. "This is the part where you say, 'We didn't catch you this time, but I'll be keeping my eye on you, boy.' Something like that."

The lieutenant gave him a steely look, but apparently didn't trust himself to say anything more. He strode out the door.

Delgado hung back, smiling.

"You shouldn't bait him, you know," he said. "It makes him mean."

"Next time I'll bring doggy treats."

The detective chuckled and shook his head. "Always the smart answer. No wonder Stanton hates you."

Sam made his eyes go round. "And I've always thought of myself as a nice guy."

"Goodnight, Mr. Hill."

"That's Mister Trickster to you."

Delgado laughed, then followed his boss outside.

18

IT WAS 7 P.M. by the time Robin Mitchell finished her research on Phil Ortiz. She dialed Sam's number, and he answered on the first ring.

"Hey," she said, "what're you doing?"

"Arranging my nuts."

"What?"

"And my bumpers."

She paused, letting it sink in. "Stanton searched you, too."

"Didn't make too much of a mess. I'm nearly finished straightening up."

"You've got a smaller inventory than I've got at the garage."

"Yeah, but more breakables. They had me worried for a while, going through all my records."

"They didn't drop any of those old blues albums you're always going on about?"

"Not a one."

"Too bad."

"Funny." Sam grunted into the phone, sounded like he was still putting things away.

"Stanton didn't find anything," she said.

"No, but he called me 'Mister Trickster.'"

"Good name for you. You should get that engraved on your belt."

Sam huffed, hamming it up. "You got information for me, or did you just call to give me a hard time?"

"I've got it. You want it over the phone?"

"Go ahead. It's all public record. But don't mention his name, just in case."

"Want the big news first?"

"Save it for last. I like to build up to it."

She smiled. "All right. That client we're talking about? He's a building contractor and he's loaded, but he has no business address. Operates everything out of a two-million-dollar house in the South Valley. No outstanding mortgage. No wife or kids. Credit report's clean. He owns chunks of businesses all over town, but always lets somebody else be the front man. Gives to South Valley charities, but he's quiet about it. You'll never see his picture in the newspaper, doing the grip-and-grin with the big check."

"So he's a good guy. Gives to charity. Looks after his mother."

"No, he's a bad guy, Sam. Newspaper says he's been called before grand juries four times in the past decade, but nothing's ever stuck to him."

"What kind of charges?"

"Drug trafficking, racketeering, assault, conspiracy to commit murder."

"A bad guy."

"Dangerous. The one photo from the newspaper shows him coming out of the courthouse, surrounded by a bunch of body-guards. Looks like one of those mob photos from back east."

"Fat guys in shiny suits."

"Exactly."

"Fascinating. Why did the grand juries let him walk?"

"Witnesses vanished. Others changed their stories."

"More scared of this guy than they were of the cops."

"Cops got to play by the rules," she said.

"Some do."

"Whatever. Guess who represented him when he was called before the grand jury."

"Who?"

"Timothy Blankenship."

"That's a familiar name. He's the attorney, owns a T-Bird."

"That's right. Blankenship represented him a couple of times, but then he disappears from the scene and our guy's got a new lawyer."

"They had a falling-out?"

"I can't tell from the records, but it fits. We know they're both car collectors, so I got an idea and ran the records on that Thunderbird. Our client was the previous owner. Probably paid off his lawyer by giving him the car."

"That would explain how he had a copy of the key."

"Right. You want the big news now?"

Sam sighed loudly. "Whatever happened to foreplay? Sure, go ahead."

"Like I said, our new friend keeps a low profile. Only time he ever comes out of his hole is when he displays his collection."

She waited for it to click. Sam said, "Car shows?"

"You got it. The guy wins all kinds of trophies for his exhibition cars. Low-riders. Chopped-down 'American Grafitti' hot rods. Fancy paint jobs, chrome trim, neon lamps, the works."

"Old cars?"

"Under there somewhere. He works them over so, they're hardly recognizable."

"I *hate* that."

"I know. Guess where he most recently showed his cars."

"How should I know?"

"Santa Fe."

After a few seconds, he got it. "On the Plaza?"

"That's the one."

"Let me guess. The guy owned a primo low-rider, a '66 Chevy Impala, green flake paint, with a large, ugly portrait of Our Lady of Guadalupe on the hood."

"Very good, Sam."

"That was *his* car?"

"I found the collection when I ran him through MVD. The guy owns like fifteen cars. One registration was flagged."

"Reported stolen," Sam said.

"That's right. Too bad, too. Seems that was his favorite."

"Naturally."

"He even posed with it for the cover photo on *Low-Rider* magazine, back in December 2001."

"The Christmas edition?"

"You got it. He wasn't dressed as baby Jesus or anything, but it was still pretty sickening."

"Praise the Lord and pass the Pepto-Bismol."

She laughed. Sam was always joking, especially when the news was bad. Robin thinking: If you were in a foxhole, you'd want to share it with Sam.

"What's he look like?" he asked.

"Kinda handsome, in a slick desperado sort of way. Got one of those short 'Miami Vice' beards. Lotta teeth."

"Big guy?"

"Medium, I think, but it's hard to tell from the photos. And I couldn't find many on the Net. Our friend doesn't get out much. For him to pose with Our Lady of Guadalupe, go public like that, the car must've been some kind of religious thing for him."

"A shrine."

"Car probably runs on holy water."

"This holy car," Sam said, "turned up missing about a month ago."

"That's right."

Robin remembered the boost well. A rich client in Santa Fe had seen the low-rider somewhere and gone ga-ga over it. Offered her prime dollar. She'd told Sam it was impossible. The streets around the capital's historic plaza were blocked off for the weekend car show. He couldn't drive a car out of there, even if he got past the tourists and the security guards. But Sam had done it. He'd called her at 3 a.m., telling her he'd swiped the prized low-rider after the guards started getting cold and sleepy and inattentive. Little damage on the front end where he'd taken out a barricade, and he bitched about how the rear bumper dragged and threw sparks every time he went over a bump in the blacktop on his way to stash it in a Santa Fe hideaway.

She smiled now, knowing Sam was reliving it, too.

"So our guy," he said, "is upset about his loss. And he decides to get even with whoever violated the Virgin Mary."

"Something like that."

"Takes him a month to track down a suspect. And he probably only succeeds because Ernesto heard about it somewhere."

"That would be my guess."

"So he gets Ernesto to set up a new situation, one involving a T-Bird. Once the job is done, he calls the cops and tries to sic them on *me*."

Robin said wryly, "How could he make such a dreadful mistake?"

"It's a puzzle. Good citizen like me, no way I'd be mixed up in something like this. And I hope all you cops who might be listening in got that part."

She laughed. "We've probably said enough over the phone."

"More than enough. But I'm glad you called. Some things are starting to make sense now."

"Seems like he's gone to a lot of trouble, just because he's mad over a stolen car."

Sam said, "Our Lady of Guadalupe works in mysterious ways."

19

SAM SLEPT LATE WEDNESDAY, despite bad dreams about cops searching through his stuff and planting evidence. Drugs and fingerprints and guns. His dreams full of guns. Most of the time Sam considered a gun a simple tool, no more exotic than a monkey wrench. Sometimes necessary, usually effective, always to be handled with care. But the guns in his nightmares were menacing and malicious. They threatened him all night, interrupted his sleep, and he awoke feeling cranky.

He puttered around his condo in his bathrobe, swilling coffee and reading the morning paper and listening to some smooth Charles Brown piano playing low on his stereo. Nothing helped. Even a shower and fresh clothes didn't improve his mood.

He kept going to the window and looking out past the hummingbird feeders at the sunny common area, with its evergreen shrubs and its spongy lawn. The sky was clear and blue, and the weather forecast called for warmer temperatures and mild breezes.

Just what I need, he thought, a warm front. That corpse can't stay in the storage unit much longer.

Finally, around lunchtime, with the sun high, he couldn't take it anymore, and he got on the phone. He let Way-Way's phone ring twenty times before the sound sleeper finally answered. Then he called Billy. They agreed to meet at Way-Way's place in half an hour.

Sam spotted the tail as soon as he steered his Caprice onto Rio Grande Boulevard, headed south. The Ford didn't have "POLICE" painted on it or gumball lights on the top, but it might as well have. Plain paint in rental-car blue, blackwall tires with no wheel covers, whip antenna on the trunk. Clearly, Stanton's boys didn't care if Sam knew he was being followed.

He slowed for a yellow light at Griegos, then blew through a quick left turn just as it slipped toward red. The Ford's tires shrieked as it braked short behind him. Somebody honked.

Sam floored it before the cops could jump the light. Griegos was a sinuous road with houses tight along its sidewalks, and he was out of sight within seconds, slaloming the Chevy through the curves.

After a mile, he braked sharply and squealed a hard right into an oblong cul-de-sac with adobe houses packed around its perimeter. Sam pulled into the second driveway, then turned around in his seat to watch Griegos.

Seconds later, the unmarked Ford zipped past the mouth of the cul-de-sac, headed east.

Sam backed the Chevy out the driveway, paused at Griegos to make sure the cops were out of view, then double-backed to the west, punching the Chevy toward Rio Grande.

He laughed. That had to be some kind of record for slipping a tail. Took him, what, a minute? Next time the cops follow him, maybe they'll be more subtle.

Sam took a circuitous route to Way-Way's house, but arrived only a few minutes late. Billy's Mustang was parked in the dirt driveway behind Way-Way's old Dodge van. Sam pulled his Chevy in behind them and tooted the horn.

Billy and Way-Way came out onto the wooden porch, and Sam smiled at the sight of them. Billy was tiny next to Way-Way, looking up at him, talking and grinning and gesturing with his twitchy hands. The little dog yapping around the big bulldog he's trying to impress.

Hard to believe those two belong to the same *species*, much less that they get along. But in the two years Billy had worked for Sam, the kid had managed to swallow his awe and become friends with the big man. Still, Billy always looked ready to scamper away, as if he feared Way-Way might lash out at any time. Or simply topple over and crush him.

They came down the steps and got into Sam's car. There was no discussion about who got the shotgun seat.

"Hiya, Sam," Billy said from the back. "Where we off to?"

"Just going for a ride. See the sights."

"Cool."

The car rocked as Way-Way slumped into his seat. Billy and Sam sat on the other side of the car as ballast, but it still felt like the Chevy leaned Way-Way's direction.

"You woke me up," Way-Way said without looking at Sam.

"You were missing a beautiful day. Sunny. Warm enough to, say, decompose a corpse."

"Think he's getting ripe?"

"He's past ripe."

Sam glanced at Billy in the rear-view. The kid's face was screwed up, and he looked pale. He wouldn't be much good around the corpse. Sam would end up with two stiffs to carry.

"So we're gonna move him?" Way-Way asked.

"Not yet."

"I figured that's why you called. I always get the heavy lifting. A woman hits on me at The Tropics, it's usually 'cause she needs help moving.'"

"You won't have to lift a thing."

"Don't get me wrong." Way-Way tilted his head to peer up at the passing skyscrapers. "I don't mind the lifting. It's the 'ripe' part I don't like."

"Gotcha."

Billy piped up from the back. "If we're not moving the body, then what are we doing?"

"Taking a look at a guy's house. Get the lay of the land."

"This Ortiz guy?"

"Yeah, him. I got his address from Robin."

"What's at his house?"

"We'll see."

Sam followed Broadway south out of downtown, taking his time, keeping an eye on his mirrors. He waved when they passed Mitch's Auto Salvage, in case Robin happened to be looking out the window. Way-Way caught the gesture and snorted.

All appeared quiet at Morelos Automotive as they passed. Sam didn't wave.

At the south end of Broadway, he steered up onto I-25 and crossed the river on a leggy bridge. The next exit was Isleta Boulevard, and Sam drove down the ramp and went north again. The South Valley was still largely agricultural, its fallow fields sliced by irrigation ditches. Little adobe houses and mobile homes, set close to the road, were inhabited by families who'd farmed the valley for generations. Here and there, bigger houses dotted the fields—mansions for the horsey set who gradually were taking over the area. After a couple of miles, Sam took a right, zig-zagging down country lanes toward the cottonwoods embracing the river. The trees still had tenacious leaves clinging to their branches, their schoolbus yellow rusting to a papery brown.

"Nice day," Way-Way grunted.

"Warm."

"I'm thinking 'ripe.'"

"So you said."

Billy made a snuffling noise in the back seat.

Sam told them about boosting the Our Lady of Guadalupe car in Santa Fe as he followed a narrow asphalt road between two faded pastures. A few brown horses loitered around, looking bored. Dried vines were snarled in the fences. Gnarly cottonwoods stood sentinel here and there, but it was mostly open land. They could see Ortiz's gray brick house from a long way off, and Sam pointed it out. A matching building, nearly as large as the house, stood a little ways distant.

"That a garage?" Way-Way asked.

"The guy shows fifteen different cars. That could hold them."

"Probably got more alarms than the White House."

"I'm not here for the garage. I want to take a look at the driveway."

The road made a couple of inexplicable bends, following fence lines, then Ortiz's driveway peeled away to the right, a swath of pristine concrete curving up to the house, which was separated from the road by thirty yards of lawn. The driveway was bracketed by a pair of brick pillars with ornamental lamps on the top. Just the kind of showy gate Sam was hoping for.

He cruised on past, watching the road, taking it slow.

"Two guys standing around in the yard, wearing sunglasses," said Way-Way, who was hunched forward to peer out the windows.

"Big guys?"

"To you, yes. To me, not so much."

"Big enough," Billy said from the back. "A Mercedes and a Chevy pickup parked out front. Driveway splits off to the right, goes around the house to the garage."

"Nice fence he's got," Way-Way said. "Looks like six-foot wrought-iron all the way around the property."

"Expensive," Sam said.

"Guy's got dough."

"Dirty money."

Way-Way turned back around in his seat as Ortiz's house fell out of sight.

"I'm guessing the fence is alarmed," he said. "Looked like flood-lights at each corner of the house. Probably more in the yard."

"This guy doesn't need prison," Sam said. "He built one for himself."

The country lane ended at a wider road, and Sam turned left, headed back toward the city.

"If this guy's got muscle hanging around," Billy said, "why doesn't he just send them after you? I mean, if he's mad because you stole his low-rider, why screw around with a dead guy and the cops and all that? If it was me, I'd just bump you off."

"Thanks."

"You know what I mean, Sam. What's this guy up to?"

Sam thought it over, not sure how to put it. Way-Way answered for him.

"Ortiz thinks he's clever. Sam stole his car, so he gets even by getting Sam to steal another one. Puts the dead guy in there for laughs."

"Making a statement," Sam said.

"Showing us how smart he is."

Sam checked his mirror, saw the twinkle in his reflection's blue eyes.

"Maybe we'll have to prove him wrong," he said.

20

THE SUN SET WHILE SAM and Billy drove to U-Stor-It-Now. Streetlights winked on and the mountains glowed red, then turned ash gray. Darkness seemed to rise up out of the ground, reaching for the first stars.

Sam dreaded opening the unit's door, but he braced himself and keyed the padlock and pushed the door up. The stench hit him and he whirled away, took a few steps, letting the odor waft away on the evening breeze.

Billy was parked thirty feet away, his Mustang pointed toward the street, the engine running. Sam gestured for him to turn off his headlights. He stood still a few seconds, listening and waiting for his eyes to adjust to the gathering darkness. The lights were out in the manager's office, leaving only the blue flicker of a television.

Sam held his breath and ducked into his storage unit, the Thunderbird's key in his hand. He was quickly behind the wheel, and he backed the car out into the parking lot and leaped out again, gasping. Left the door open. Gave the aroma some room.

He locked up the garage, then gave Billy a wave before jumping back behind the wheel of the Stenchmobile.

He powered down all the windows as he drove the car onto San Mateo Boulevard. The cold air stung his face, but it smelled better than the dead guy. He drove as fast as the speed limit allowed, imagining that the car left a visible, noxious cloud in its wake.

Sam wore gloves and his leather jacket was zipped up tight against the chill. A pistol bulged against his chest in the jacket's inside pocket.

Traffic was light, and he made good time, keeping an eye on Billy's Mustang behind him. By the time they turned onto Phil Ortiz's isolated country road, Billy's were the only headlights in view.

Sam slowed to a crawl as he steered through the two bends that preceded Ortiz's place. Lights glowed in the windows, and a couple of cars were parked near the front door, but no one stood guard at the driveway's gate.

Sam killed the T-Bird's lights and turned in, stopping the low-slung car at an angle, so its fenders practically touched the brick pillars on either side of the driveway. He shut off the engine and set the parking brake. He jumped out, locked the doors, hurled the key as far as he could into a pasture. Then he sprinted for Billy's car.

Billy had the door open when Sam got there, and they were under way in seconds. Sam watched the house as they passed, but no new lights came on, no one came running. Wouldn't be long, though, before somebody noticed the T-Bird blocking the driveway like a big gold brick.

Billy gunned his engine, and the house quickly was out of sight.

"Smooth," he said.

"Now comes the fun part."

Sam pulled a cell phone from a jacket pocket and dialed the police emergency number. The dispatcher who answered had a voice like a power drill.

"Hello, police?" Sam said. "I want to report a murder."

The dispatcher started droning a bunch of questions, but Sam talked over her.

"There's a car, an old gold Thunderbird. Smells terrible. I think someone's dead in it."

Rapid-fire questions again.

Sam reeled off Ortiz's address, then said, "It's out in the county, near Isleta Boulevard." He repeated the address. Then he hung up.

When Sam looked over at Billy, the kid's crooked face was split by a big grin.

"We gave him some of his own medicine?"

"A big dose."

"You could've told me, Sam. I didn't know what the hell you were up to. I saw you were packing. Thought you were going to shoot up the place or something, *then* dump the car."

"This way's plenty. Cops'll be crawling all over it in minutes."

"Still. You shoulda told me."

"More fun to keep you in the dark. Were you *scared*?"

"Who, me?

21

SAM STAYED OUT LATE Wednesday night, drinking beer with Billy at The Tropics, maintaining an alibi. They told Way-Way about their prank with the Thunderbird, and the bouncer rumbled his approval.

Getting back at Phil Ortiz allowed Sam to sleep peacefully. Or maybe it was the beers. Whichever, it took him a full minute to come awake Thursday morning and register that his phone was ringing.

The answering machine offered to take a message. A few seconds later, the ringing started up again. Somebody punching "redial" until Sam got out of bed. He had a pretty good idea who was calling.

He took his time. He put on his bathrobe and brushed his teeth and started the coffee to perking. The fourth time the ringing pattern repeated, he picked up.

"Good morning."

"A good morning? No, I don't think so. A good day to die, maybe?"

"Phil Ortiz?"

"Don't say names."

"We meet at last," Sam said. "I was wondering when you'd call."

"I would've called sooner, you son of a bitch, but I just got home. I've been downtown all night with sheriff's deputies and lawyers."

"Run into a legal problem?"

"Oh, it's no problem. Nothing to tie me to that car. I don't own it anymore. No reason for some asshole to leave it blocking my driveway."

"With that fence all around your property," Sam said, "I guess there's no other way to drive out, huh? The cops show up, and you're trapped in your own cage."

Ortiz grumbled. Sam didn't know much Spanish, but he was pretty sure they were curse words. He'd heard them before.

"So what did you tell the cops?" Sam said. "The guy in the trunk, he drove himself there?"

"The police are … excitable." Ortiz seemed to savor the word. "It was just a matter of waiting them out. They've got no evidence against me. That car was reported stolen. Anyone could've left it here."

"They search your place?"

"Yes, but of course they found nothing. Tried to pressure me, but eventually gave it up because they've got *nada*."

"Too bad. Bet there's lots you could've told them about that corpse."

A silence. Sam guessed the man was getting himself under control.

"I could've told them *your* name," Ortiz said, "but I saw no profit in it."

"No, what you saw was the buttload of trouble I could bring your way. You drop my name, I mention yours, pretty soon everybody's got problems."

"I assure you," Ortiz said, "your problems would be much greater than mine."

"Maybe."

"Let's say yours would be more *final*."

Sam let that sink in. "What do you say we call it even? You had your little fun. I had mine. So far, nothing's sticking to anybody. We ought to keep it that way."

Ortiz made him wait. Sam stood holding the phone, staring out the window at the hummingbirds darting around in the sunshine.

"I don't think we're even," Ortiz said finally. "You're forgetting who drew first blood here. There's the matter of a certain car that belongs to me."

"Ah, Our Lady of Guadalupe. I was wondering when we'd get around to that."

"I want that car back."

"Impossible."

"Wrong answer. This is not just about a car, though I admit that one is special to me. This is a matter of honor. No one steals from me and gets away with it."

Sam had to bite his tongue. A matter of honor. Such bullshit. It's a *car*. And as such, it was made to be stolen by anyone ballsy enough to drive it away. That's why they have *wheels* on them.

"Return the car and maybe we can work out the rest."

"Not gonna happen. I don't even know where the car is."

Ortiz's voice was low and cold. "That's too bad. Because you won't like what happens next."

22

SAM ARRIVED EARLY for the pow-wow. The Monte Carlo Steak-
house is one of those joints the tourists never find, though it's right
on Route 66 just west of the river. Place looks like a package store
from the street—which it is—but the restaurant in back is popular
for its grilled beef and man-sized drinks and outrageous décor.

Décor, Sam mused as he waited for a table, might be too tame
a word. Every inch of the open, windowless room was decorated
in some way, none of it matching anything else, as if the owners
started collecting stuff when the restaurant opened thirty-some
years earlier and had never thrown out anything since. Model car
collections filled glass cabinets along one wall. Elvis memorabilia
on another set of shelves. Decorative liquor decanters in another
case. Photos and pennants and gimcracks everywhere. Curling
business cards thumb-tacked to the rough wooden walls.

Checkered tabletops were weighed down with steaks and burg-
ers and bowls of chili. A waitress hustled past with a tray held high,
carrying a huge tenderloin right past Sam's nose. He inhaled deeply,
and thought of Way-Way. This was his kind of place—big platters
of meat. Maybe a nice meal would placate Way-Way. He hadn't
been happy about getting awakened by Sam three days in a row.

The lunch rush was winding down, but most of the tables still
were full. Sam settled into a booth near the model car collection
just as Way-Way and Billy showed up. A hush fell over the room
as Way-Way ducked under a beer banner hanging from the ceiling. Billy squirted between tables, leaving Way-Way to squeeze
through behind him without accidentally hurting anybody.

"Place is busy," Way-Way said as he fell into the booth. Murmured
conversation resumed in the restaurant, but people still stared.

Way-Way, as usual, didn't seem to notice the awe that followed him everywhere.

Billy was pinned between Way-Way and the wall, and it looked as if the little guy didn't have room to breathe.

"Be careful what you say," Sam said. "Lotta cops eat in this place. You never know who's at the next table."

Billy nodded and glanced around, like he might recognize undercover cops in every booth. It made Sam smile.

His smile widened when he spotted Robin weaving between tables, coming toward them. Her hair was down and she wore a peach-colored blouse with a ruffled front, jeans, and high heels. She looked great, and another little hush-and-murmur followed in her wake.

"You folks sure know how to make an entrance," Sam said as she sat next to him.

"We coulda met someplace quiet," Way-Way said.

"No, I like this. Loud, busy, cops all around. Right out in the public eye."

Robin said, "You need an alibi for something?"

"Not at the moment, but you never know."

An out-of-breath waitress stopped by long enough to dump off oversized menus. Way-Way rested his big forearms on the table, which tipped and nearly sent all the salt shakers and condiment bottles into Billy's lap.

They made adjustments, which resulted in Billy being squeezed even tighter against the wall. Sam thought Billy might have to eat through a straw. After they looked over the menus, Way-Way said, "The twenty-ounce porterhouse looks good."

"Twenty ounces!" Robin said. "Are you kidding me? I could live a week on that."

"I thought about something bigger," he said, "but this is breakfast for me."

On cue, the waitress showed up with coffee, and they all sugared and stirred and waited for Sam to start the meeting.

"You're probably wondering why I called you all here today," he said.

Billy said, "Funny." The other two gave him the usual deadpan.

"I got a call this morning from our new friend, the car collector. He's not a happy man."

Robin gave Sam a suspicious look. "Why's that?"

"Somebody wedged a '65 Thunderbird in his driveway last night." Sam kept his voice just above a whisper. "The police came to check it out, found a stiff. Ortiz was up all night, being grilled by the cops."

"I love it when you talk like a gangster movie," she said.

"Stop it," Way-Way said. "You're making me blush."

Robin ignored him. "You told me you were going to give *me* that T-Bird."

"Oops," Sam said. "I forgot. Sorry. Believe me, you wouldn't want that car. No way to get the smell out."

Billy made a face. "Can we get back to the point? The guy's unhappy about the T-Bird. He called. What did he *want*?"

"He wanted to share his unhappiness with me. I told him, hey, we're even now, but he doesn't see it that way. He wants the Our Lady car back."

"Get outta here," Robin said.

"I told him we don't do business that way."

"Damned straight," she said.

"He said, if he doesn't get that car back, I won't like what happens next."

"No specifics?" Anticipation in Way-Way's voice told Sam he was hoping for something gory.

"No, but I don't think we're talking about practical jokes anymore."

"So what are you going to do?" Billy asked.

Before Sam could answer, Way-Way said, "We go over to this guy's place and I pull off his head."

"You want to keep it down?" Billy said tightly. "You can't talk about pulling people's heads off in restaurants. It's not polite, right, Sam?"

"It would seem to be a breach of table etiquette, William. Besides, I don't think we're at the pulling-off-heads stage yet."

Robin said, "There's a 'pulling-off-heads stage?'"

"We've got a plan for everything," Sam said. "Way-Way usually votes for dismemberment."

"It's quick," the big man said. "It's easy. Not a lot of second-guessing."

The waitress turned up again, and Sam ordered a sirloin. Billy opted for a green-chile cheeseburger. Way-Way requested what sounded like a small steer. Robin ordered a salad, which made the others hoot and jeer.

She glowered at them until they finished hiccupping and wiping their eyes. Then she said, "What are you going to do, Sam?"

"I'm not sure yet. Suggestions?"

"Lay low," Billy said.

"That's an option, William. And it's 'lie' low, not 'lay.'"

Way-Way raised a beefy hand. "Why do you keep calling him William?"

"Didn't he tell you? It's William now. Billy sounds too juvenile."

Way-Way ran a hand over his glinting head and twisted around so he could look at the kid sandwiched beside him.

"Is that right?"

Billy blushed furiously. "I've been rethinking that, Sam. I mean, everyone's used to—"

"No, I *like* William," Way-Way said. "Maybe even Willie."

"Willie's good," Sam said.

"Billy's fine. Really. So are you going to *lie* low or what?"

"For how long?" Sam said. "This guy tracked me down once. He'll do it again. I'm supposed to just sit around, waiting for him?"

"You should've thought about that before you played your joke on him," Robin said.

"Just a little eye-for-an-eye," Sam said.

"These things have a way of escalating," she said. "Next, it's teeth, as I recall. Before you know it, a bunch of blind, toothless guys are hurting each other."

"What would you suggest?"

"Take a vacation. Go to Vegas for a week or two. We'll keep an ear to the ground here, see if things settle down. For all we know, the cops can link Ortiz to the dead guy. Maybe they'll arrest him and he'll be too busy being in jail to worry about you anymore."

"This guy's plugged in. He might hear where I went. Then I'm on unfamiliar ground, watching over my shoulder—"

"How would he find out? You register under a false name. Don't you have a whole drawer full of fake IDs somewhere?"

Sam did indeed. In a safe deposit box at a neighborhood bank. But he shook his head.

"I don't like leaving a mess behind. And I'm not done with Ernesto yet."

"You're going after Ernesto and Ortiz both?"

Sam glanced around the room. No one was eavesdropping. "I'd rather not. But Ernesto should be punished, don't you think?"

"Didn't you and Way-Way put the fear into him already? You almost killed that old guy."

"What old guy?"

"Moe. Worked in Ernesto's office. He had a heart attack when you two went busting in there. One of the other salvage dealers told me about it on the phone today."

"I remember that geezer," Sam said. "I thought maybe he always looked like that. He in bad shape?"

"They saved him in the ambulance, but he's in the hospital, maybe forever."

"Too bad."

"I hear Ernesto's mad as hell. Without his documents guy, he's screwed."

"Maybe *he'll* try to get even with me, too."

"Ernesto's too chicken. He'll never cross you again."

"I think he's more scared of Ortiz. Everybody else seems to be."

"That's what this is about, isn't it?" Her voice grew chilly. "You don't like Ortiz. He's dirty money. He's a big shot. Everybody's scared of him. You can't stand it, can you? A man like that, you've got to tweak him some way—"

"I thought we were talking about Ernesto."

"I can fix Ernesto. I'll never do business with that dirtbag again. And I'll put out the word to the other dealers. Cut him off."

Sam thought it over, then said, "Not good enough."

"Why not?"

"Because I wouldn't be there to see it. Ernesto's got that great sweaty face. I want to fix him in a way I can witness it."

"You just want to gloat."

"Whatever."

"Ernesto's not going anywhere. You can get even with him after you get back to town."

"I'm not leaving. For all I know, I skip out and they'll torch my house or something."

"So it's better," she said, "that Ortiz should burn down your house while you're in it?"

"He can try. But he might get more than he bargained for."

The puffing waitress arrived again, this time carrying so much chow that her tray sagged under the weight. They sat quietly while she dispensed the food, most of it ending up in front of Way-Way. He immediately began sawing away at his bloody steak and cramming huge hunks into his mouth. Stoking the engine.

"If you won't leave town," Robin said, "at least stay someplace else for a few days. Stay at Way-Way's."

"He only has one bed."

"You could sleep on the weight bench," Way-Way said around a mouthful of meat.

"Stay at the garage," Robin said. "I'll give you a key. The couch in the office is pretty comfortable. You could sleep there."

"I've already got a key."

"Really?"

"Your dad gave me one years ago."

"Wonder how many more are floating around? Maybe I should change the locks."

"Maybe I'll just sleep at my own place," Sam said. "I'd rather keep an eye on it."

"I'll watch it for you, Sam," Billy said.

"No, that's okay. I may need you for something else."

"Want me to go hurt Ernesto?"

"William! I'm surprised at you."

Billy blushed.

"Anybody gets to hurt Ernesto, it's me," Way-Way said, pointing at his chest with his fork. "I hate that guy."

"You hate everybody."

"Some more than others. Ernesto's on top of the list." That said, Way-Way went back to carving up his cow.

"Couldn't we work it out so that nobody gets hurt?" Robin said. "Ernesto's not worth the trouble. And Ortiz might reconsider."

"Maybe," Sam said. "But I got a feeling things are gonna get weirder."

"And you wouldn't miss it for the world," she said.

Sam grinned at her. "It'll be fine."

"So you called us here," she said. "Asked our advice. Now you're not going to take any of it."

"It's good advice. I needed to hear it. But I don't want to turn tail and run yet. The cops are all over Ortiz now. He won't try anything while they're watching."

"They won't watch forever," she said.

"Maybe we can speed things along before they lose interest."

Robin stared into his eyes for a long moment, then said, "You need to be careful. I don't want you getting hurt."

Way-Way's laugh boomed and they turned to find him pointing at them with his greasy knife.

"You two are so cute together."

That killed the conversation.

23

SAM WENT TO BED EARLY Thursday night, but slept fitfully, starting awake to every imagined noise, a pistol beside his pillow. Phil Ortiz didn't come for him. They were back to the waiting game.

When he awoke Friday, his mind was on the cops, whether they were making a case against Ortiz for the death of Antonio Armas. It would be sweet if the police got Ortiz off the streets. Make things a little safer for Sam. Plus, it would be the ultimate payoff from the stunt he'd pulled with the T-Bird. One for the record books.

He'd showered and dressed and was having more coffee when the doorbell rang. He peeked out the narrow window beside the door, and saw a petite, well-dressed black woman and a big white guy in a Western-cut suit. Not goons sent by Ortiz. Not Stanton's people.

Sam flung open the door and said, "Good morning. You must be with the Drug Enforcement Administration."

The man's gray eyes widened briefly, then his jaw set and he nodded and pulled out an ID. "Agent Quincy Brock. And this is my partner, Agent Rhetta Jones. You were expecting us?"

"Everyone else has shown up lately. I figured it was your turn. Come on in."

They followed him into the living room, Jones' low heels clacking on the brick floor.

"Coffee?"

"No, thanks. We just need a few minutes of your time."

The agents shared the sofa. Sam sat in an armchair across from them and sized them up. Brock wore black roper boots and had the sun-leathered face of a cowboy. Late forties, a little gray at the temples of his short brown hair. Jones had skin the color of pecan pie and straightened hair and rabbity teeth she kept hidden behind pursed lips. Her horn-rimmed glasses made her look like an accountant. Sam gave her a smile, but she looked away, waiting for her partner to take the lead.

"APD got a tip," Brock said, "that you were somehow involved with a suspected drug dealer named Phil Ortiz."

Sam kept his face blank. "Never heard of him."

Brock frowned, then dug a notebook out of his pocket and flipped pages until he found what he wanted.

"You ever hear of a 1965 Ford Thunderbird, gold paint, fully restored? Showed up night before last at the home of Mr. Ortiz?"

"No."

"There was a body in the trunk of that car, Mr. Hill. A man named Antonio Armas."

"You mean a *dead* body?"

Brock pressed his lips together. Sam sensed it might be better not to joke with this guy. The feds get you in their sights, you can disappear into the system a long time.

"I don't know anything about that, Agent Brock."

"Then why would we hear that you did?"

"Where did you hear it? Lieutenant Stanton?"

Brock hesitated, then nodded.

"Figures. Guy has it in for me. He searched my place, took me downtown for questioning, won't tell me what it's about. Now he sics you two on me. Where did Stanton get this tip? Did he say?"

"It was anonymous," the woman said. She shot her partner an I-told-you-so look that made Sam think they hadn't been too impressed with Stanton.

Brock scooted forward on the sofa and rested his elbows on his knees. Locked eyes with Sam.

"I might be inclined to believe," Brock said, "that Lieutenant Stanton's using us because he's got a grudge. But we'd already heard your name in connection with Mr. Armas' disappearance."

"Another anonymous tip?"

Brock ignored the question. "Then yesterday something else came up."

"What's that?"

"After the body was reported, we checked Mr. Ortiz's phone records," Brock said.

"If he's a drug dealer, I'm surprised you don't have him tapped."

Brock's lipless mouth twitched. "We didn't have probable cause until that body showed up. But we know that somebody at Ortiz's house called your number repeatedly yesterday morning. Like five times. What was that about, Mr. Hill?"

"Beats me. I didn't get any calls."

"Your phone rings five different times, and you don't answer it? Don't hear it? Not once?"

"Maybe it was a malfunction."

Brock snorted and studied the toes of his boots. His partner took up the questioning.

"Mr. Hill." She had a voice like a telephone operator. "You didn't know Antonio Armas?"

"The guy in the trunk?"

She nodded primly.

"Never heard of him. Who was he?"

"A nobody," Brock said, looking up. "Junkie. Small-time hood. But he was facing an assault rap, his third strike, and we turned him."

"An informant."

"That's right. We got him a job in Ortiz's construction company, then started moving him over into the drug trade. It was slow, and Tony wasn't exactly reliable, but he was getting close. He was wearing a wire for us when somebody shot him in the head."

"You heard it happen?"

"No. He was on a tape recorder, gathering evidence."

"Did you recover the tape?" Sam asked.

Brock shook his head.

"Too bad."

"Go tell it to Tony's family."

Something hot had come into Brock's voice. His partner's hand shot out and rested on his arm. It seemed to have a calming effect.

"I think you know about this," Brock said evenly. "And I think we can put you in that car. A fingerprint. A fiber. A hair. Doesn't take much these days. Not with DNA testing. We put you in that car, and you become our number one suspect in this murder."

"How's that possible? I didn't even know the dead guy. I don't know this Ortiz either. Who'd ever believe I was mixed up with them?"

Brock sat back, and he and Jones looked at each other. Brock might be right about some minuscule evidence left in the T-Bird, but they didn't have it yet. Sam could see it in their faces.

"Maybe we're approaching this all wrong," Jones said. "You say you don't know Ortiz. Maybe we *want* you to know him. If you got close to him—"

"You could put a wire on *me*. And I'd be the next dead guy found in some car."

"We could protect you," Brock said. "We could set it up—"

"Forget it. No way I become your informant. Not with your recent track record."

Brock's hands wrestled with each other. They were big, knobby hands. Outdoor hands. Sam wondered what Brock did before he donned a suit for the DEA.

Sam changed the subject. "You said this Ortiz owns a construction company. He a rich guy?"

Agent Jones nodded.

"Then why's he messing around with drugs? Why doesn't he make his money legitimately?"

"Because he can wholesale heroin for fifteen-hundred dollars an ounce," she said. "No legit business pays that well."

Sam said nothing, thinking it over.

"You ever seen black tar heroin?" Jones asked. "Ever seen what it does to a person?"

Sam shook his head.

"Junkies on black tar don't eat, and they waste away to nothing. The withdrawal is murder—vomiting, shakes, sweats, cramps. It's like the worse case of flu you can imagine. So they keep popping it. Their livers get diseased. Their kidneys shut down. They get clogged veins that damage other organs. They're so sick, they can barely move around enough to rob your nice house to get the money for their next fix."

"And Ortiz deals this stuff?"

"Among other things," Brock said. "Black tar's epidemic in northern New Mexico right now. It's everywhere in Espanola, Chimayo, Santa Fe. It's eating people up. We think Phil Ortiz is the man moving it up from western Mexico."

"But you can't prove anything," Sam said, "or you wouldn't be sitting here."

"That's why we're asking for your help," she said.

Sam shook his head and got to his feet, put a little distance between himself and Brock.

"This guy needs locking up, then I wish you all the best. But I'm not playing."

The color rose in Brock's face, but his partner tapped him on the arm again, and they stood up.

"These junkies," Brock said. "Their life is hell."

"I'm sorry."

"We could make your life hell, too, Mr. Hill. If that's what it takes."

"Better bring it on then. Because I'm not wearing a wire for you."

The two men stared at each other until Jones stepped between them and thanked Sam for his time. She gave him her business card.

"If you change your mind, call us," she said. "We can work together to put this man behind bars."

"Not gonna happen."

He saw the agents to the door. They didn't look happy, but they didn't try to play him further. He watched out the window as they went past, the woman's mouth going, undoubtedly giving her partner another lecture on anger management. Then they were gone around the corner toward the parking lot.

Sam knew he'd see them again. Which made his unresolved business with Phil Ortiz even more urgent.

24

THE FEDS HAD BEEN GONE two minutes when Sam's doorbell rang. He opened the door and found Joe Winter staring up at him through his thick glasses. The condo manager's white hair was askew, and his face was flushed.

"Hey, Joe."

"Those more cops?"

"Feds."

"I thought so. I recognize the type. Cocksuckers."

"What have you got against cops?"

"I used to have my little run-ins with the law. Now and then. Man's got to make a living. 'Course, that was before I got older than God's baby teeth."

Sam laughed, but Joe's face turned somber.

"I understand about cops coming around, sticking their noses in people's business," Joe said. "Up to me, I wouldn't say a word to you about it. You've always treated us well. Paid your bills on time."

"Somebody complain?"

"A couple of your neighbors, asking about the 'police activity' at your place. I told them to mind their own business, but they didn't like that answer. You know how it is. They worry. Some of 'em have their life savings tied up in these units. They don't want bad publicity—"

"I understand completely. I don't want cops coming around either. They stink up the place."

Joe squinted up at him. "You got problems? Anything I can help you with?"

"No, it's all a big misunderstanding. It'll get straightened out soon."

"You know me, Sam. I never ask questions. Never asked you what you do for a living, even. I wonder about it sometimes, but I mind my own business."

"I appreciate that, Joe."

"It's just that the tenants, when they complain, I have to do something."

"Right. I'd expect you to do the same for me, if I were the kind of fucking rat who complained about his neighbors."

Joe grinned at him. "I'm glad we understand each other."

The old man started to leave, then turned back. "You need any help, Sam, you call me."

"Thanks, Joe."

Sam watched him totter off, straight across the manicured lawn, leaving big damp footprints behind.

"Goddammit," Sam muttered as he shut the door.

He crossed the living room, looking around at the bookshelves and the record collection and the cushiony furniture. A comfortable place. Quiet. Simple.

He'd hate to move. But he couldn't afford neighbors who were watching him all the time, waiting for the next episode of *COPS*. He needed to get the police out of his life. Let it all settle down, then see whether he could stay here.

He felt edgy and confined. Too many pressures coming from too many directions. He closed his eyes and took a deep breath.

When he opened his eyes, he saw clearly again: All this turmoil centers on Phil Ortiz. Get him out of the picture, and the feds, the cops, the corpses, the nosy neighbors all go away. Eventually.

But how to make Phil Ortiz disappear? Set him up for the DEA? Let Way-Way pull his head off?

Might be simplest to just go up to Santa Fe, find the Our Lady of Guadalupe low-rider, steal it, and return it to Ortiz. Perhaps if the guy got his sainted car he'd go away, and everybody could get back to their quiet businesses.

But stealing from a client went against Sam's grain. He'd have to get Robin involved. The cops were all over him already.

And, car or no car, it was probably too late now to smooth things over with Phil Ortiz.

25

SAM MADE A FEW CALLS, but mostly he hung around indoors, feeling low. He ate a ham sandwich for lunch, and was mopily cleaning up the dishes when his doorbell rang again.

"Busy day," he said as he dried his hands. He crossed the condo to the front door and looked out the glass, then jerked his head back out of sight. He'd seen all he needed to see at a glance. Three tough-looking men waited outside, dressed in jeans and jackets and boots. Two were standard-issue fat ass thugs, crowding in behind their boss. The leader was short and broad-shouldered, with reddish-brown hair and a lumpy face and gunfighter eyes. He held a three-foot length of lead pipe close beside his leg.

Everything Sam saw in that glimpse—but especially that hunk of pipe—clicked in his head and he wheeled and ran for his bedroom and the pistol stashed there.

The door crashed open behind him. Feet slapped the brick floors as the three men chased him across the living room and down the short hall.

Sam reached the drawer in the bedside table as the pipe cracked across the backs of his knees, taking his legs out from under him. He bounced off his bed and onto the floor, rolling away just as a boot whished past his head.

He scrambled to his feet, but his legs weren't working properly and he stumbled and fell sideways against a wall. The leader swung for Sam's head and the pipe thudded into the plaster when he ducked away.

The two bigger men managed to squeeze into the bedroom and one of them—a beefy Navajo with short, grimy hair—made a grab for Sam, got hold of his shirt. Sam twisted in his grasp, ducked under the Indian's thick arm, and sank a left hook into his mid-section. The Navajo suddenly forgot what he was doing, too busy gasping for air.

The pipe sang again and Sam dodged left, just in time to see the errant swing crease the Navajo across the forehead. Bong. The big man slumped to the floor. The redhead cursed and spat on the Indian, then danced around him, the pipe raised high, ready to swing at Sam's head, try to knock it out of the ballpark.

The other big man, a thick-bodied bruiser with an ornate "2" tat-tooed on the side of his neck, moved to Sam's left, keeping him cornered. Worse, he blocked access to the bedside table. The gun in that drawer was Sam's only hope.

He had his legs under him now. The guy with the pipe was clos-ing in. No question about which way to move.

Sam shouted and leaped toward the tattooed bruiser, who instinctively threw up his arms to protect himself. Sam kicked up, caught the man on the kneecap. The fat man winced and grabbed for his knee. Sam hooked him one in the jaw, then spun him out of the way, diving toward the bedside table.

As he yanked open the drawer, something popped loudly against the back of his head, and he saw a flash of bright white light. Then nothing.

26

PHIL ORTIZ ORDERED the heavy drapes shut over the windows at each end of his huge garage, so the only light came from hooded shop lamps that dangled from the pitched ceiling. The glare cast shadows around the room, made it feel like night rather than sunny afternoon. Night felt right for the work he was about to do.

Phil washed his hands at a steel sink set into a cabinet along one wall of the spotless garage. He checked his face in the chrome-rimmed mirror above the sink, searching for some sign of cruelty, some hint of anxiety, but he found only the usual passive good looks.

His face bore high cheekbones and features he thought of as "patrician." His hair swept back from a widow's peak above a forehead unwrinkled by worry. The smoothness offset the manicured stubble on his jaw, which gave him a rough edge.

He was, in his way, a work of art, as much as the restored cars that surrounded him. Phil prayed often, but at least once a day he gave thanks to God that he'd been blessed with this face rather than a nasty mug like most of the men he knew.

He turned now to find three particularly ugly ones staring at him, waiting. Deuce, with his fat jowls and his muddy tattoos and his brain the size of a jalapeño. Albert, the square-jawed Navajo, still glassy-eyed from the fight at Hill's, a ridge of bruising flesh above his eyebrows. And Johnny Murdoch, with his sandstone face and his weathered eyes.

Murdoch still held his stupid length of pipe. Phil already scolded him for the way he'd handled the pick-up of Sam Hill. Carrying a fucking pipe around, making a lot of noise, whacking Albert by accident. Murdoch could've accomplished the same thing quietly, with a gun, but he always preferred the primitive.

If Murdoch had been smart about this, Sam Hill would be awake now, instead of curled up in the back seat of Deuce's car, out cold. And Phil could get on with his business.

It's my own fault, he thought. I told Murdoch to bring Sam Hill to me, but I didn't specify how I wanted it done. I've got to learn that I can't leave details up to Murdoch. The pug keeps making mistakes. Putting Armas in the trunk. Knocking out Sam Hill when I want him awake to talk.

"Bring him," he said.

Deuce limped over to his Dodge, parked just inside the garage doors for secrecy. Phil looked over the dusty car, hoped it wouldn't leak oil on his concrete floor.

Deuce opened the back door, grabbed Hill by the collar of his black denim shirt and dragged him out of the seat. Hill's limp legs tumbled from the car and his feet hit the floor with a whap. Deuce got a better grip on him, collar and belt, and dragged him over to where the rest of them waited.

Murdoch put his pipe aside and fetched a metal folding chair, one with rubber feet to protect the floor. Deuce draped Hill over the chair. The unconscious thief tried to slither off onto the floor.

"Help him, Albert," Phil said, and the two big men managed to hold Hill in place. "Wake him up, Johnny."

Murdoch stepped around the others to get at Hill. He grabbed the man's tangled blond hair and lifted up his head. Hill's eyes were closed and his mouth hung open wetly. Murdoch slapped one cheek, then backhanded the other. A couple more slaps, and Hill blinked and coughed and tried to focus his eyes. He jerked his head back and looked around, taking in the men all around him and the glaring lights overhead.

Phil slipped a shop apron over his head and cinched it tight around his waist. He didn't want to get blood on his designer clothes.

"Mr. Hill," he said. "Are you back among the living?"

Hill said nothing, but there was a spark in his blue eyes. He was awake.

"I have some questions for you," Phil said. "You'll answer them immediately and completely. Any lies, any hesitation, will mean pain for you. Do you understand?"

Hill met his eyes and nodded warily.

"Today you were visited by two agents of the DEA," Phil said. "I sent my friends here to pick you up earlier, and they spotted the feds at your place. Brock and a woman."

Hill said nothing. Phil leaned over and slapped him across the cheek. The car thief winced, then his face went blank.

"Answer me," Phil said.

"You didn't ask a question."

"What?"

"You *told* me the DEA came to see me. It wasn't a question. You want to know something, you should ask."

Phil grabbed the thief by the ear and twisted fiercely. Hill tried to leap up from the chair, but Albert and Deuce held tightly to his arms. Hill clamped his teeth together and growled against the pain.

After a few seconds, Phil let go and stepped back. Hill blew his breath out in rapid puffs. His ear was bright red. He settled onto his chair. Deuce and Albert relaxed, and Hill lunged forward, nearly got to Phil before the big men grabbed him and shoved him roughly into the chair.

"He seems—" Phil searched for the right word, found it. "—defiant. Soften him up, Johnny."

Phil moved out of the way as Murdoch eagerly stepped up to the man in the chair. Hill tried to jump up again, but the other two had him firmly now. Murdoch unleashed a low punch that caught Hill in the midsection and forced the wind out of him. Before he could recover, Murdoch hit him in the ribs, then hard with another raw-boned right, just below the heart.

Hill went limp, gasping for air. Murdoch waited a moment, letting Hill catch his breath. Then he hit him again with the same combination.

"Johnny used to be a boxer," Phil said. "A Golden Gloves champ. After he turned pro, they called him Murderin' Murdoch. He knows how to use his hands."

Phil turned away, looking over the shiny brass trophies in a glass case against the wall, while Murdoch went to work again.

After a minute, Deuce said, "He's out."

"Okay, Johnny," Phil said without turning around. "That's enough. Wake him up."

It took a while, but the thief finally came around. Phil stood over him.

"You ready to tell me now? About the DEA?"

Hill swallowed heavily and nodded.

"Brock and his partner came to my place, but I didn't call them. This APD lieutenant, Stanton, auto theft guy, has a hard-on for me. He tipped them that I had something to do with that Thunderbird. They had questions."

"About me?"

"Mostly."

"And how did you answer them?"

"Told 'em I'd never heard of you. Which raises some interesting questions if they find out I'm here now."

"Do *you* even know where you are?"

"Your place, right? This your car collection? I can't see much of it for all the tarps, but it's a nice garage. Clean."

Phil let himself feel a moment of pride before he got back to the point. "Did Brock believe you?"

"He tried to lean on me. Said he'd place me in that T-Bird, find some DNA evidence. Pin the Armas murder on me, when you and I both know I didn't do it."

Hill smirked, and Phil smiled back, playing along. Then he slapped Hill's face.

"Don't get smart," Phil said. "It makes me mad. Believe me, you don't want me any madder than I am already."

"I don't know why you're so angry. I told the DEA nothing. They wanted me to rat you out, wear a wire, all that, but I refused."

Phil glanced at Murdoch.

"We searched him before we hauled him out of his place," Murdoch said. "He's not wired."

"Of course," Phil said.

"Bet that's what he said about Armas, too," Hill said.

Murdoch snarled and tried to take another whack at Sam Hill, but Phil pushed him away.

"Don't let him bait you, Johnny. He thinks he's smart. We'll see how he feels at the end of the day."

The car thief glared at him. "You think the cops don't know I'm here? They've been following me. I have to shake a tail every time I leave the house. They're watching you, too."

Phil felt anger well up within him. "They weren't, not until you parked that T-Bird at my house."

"They were already all over you. Brock said they had Armas in place for months, trying to get close to you, wearing a wire. They've tapped your phone. You're number one on their Hit Parade."

Surprised, Phil said, "My phone?"

"That's what Brock said. And if they're listening to your phone, maybe they've wired this garage, too. They searched the place the other night, after they found Armas' body, right? Lot of fender wells in here where somebody could hide a bug."

Phil glanced around the room at the hooded cars. He needed to get the place swept for bugs. And soon. The thought that the feds might be using his garage, his sanctuary, to do their snooping, made him uneasy.

"Maybe I should just finish you quickly and quietly," Phil said, his voice low. "Get this over with, clean up the mess."

"Gonna seem awfully suspicious to the DEA. One informant gets killed. They try to recruit another guy and he disappears the same day."

"They'll think you skipped town. You were frightened of them. Of me. You ran away."

Hill shook his head. "You make me disappear, and they'll know. You can't afford any more heat right now."

"Don't tell me what I can 'afford.'" Phil's mind was working over-time, calculating odds and risks and needs.

"I have only one reason to keep you alive," he said finally. "My car. Our Lady of Guadalupe. You can recover it for me."

"I told you—"

Phil slugged him in the jaw and immediately regretted it. It hurt his hand. Hurt Hill worse, though. His head bobbed around on his neck, and bloody spittle dripped from the corner of his mouth.

"I want that car back. You think I won't kill you, but there are worse things than dying. Pain, for instance. I can give you pain for a long time. I'm a creative guy. I poke enough holes in you, and you'll be begging for the opportunity to return my car."

Hill took a shuddering breath. "Maybe I could get it back."

Phil straightened up and put his throbbing hand in the pocket of his apron.

"I knew you'd see it my way," he said. "Do a good job. Because my car, it just became your only reason for living."

Hill said nothing.

"Don't talk to the DEA. Don't run to the cops. Try it, and you're a dead man. Go get my car, bring it back in one piece, maybe you reach a ripe old age."

Phil turned away, began removing his apron.

"You three take Mr. Hill for a ride in the country. Make sure you're not followed. Take your time with him, but don't break any bones. He needs to be in good shape again soon."

Phil looked back at Hill, who struggled against the big men, venom in his eyes.

"He's got a car to steal."

27

SAM DRAGGED HIS FEET and twisted his arms, but the two goons' grasp was unyielding as they hustled him across the yard to a beat-up truck. Johnny Murdoch got behind the wheel.

Sam had a moment of hope as they tossed him into the bed of the pickup. In an open truck, he could jump out somewhere, make a run for it, start yelling his ass off.

But the Navajo shoved Sam to the floor of the truck bed, face down, and sat on his back. He wiggled around, making himself comfortable, as the truck shot forward. Sam couldn't move. He could barely breathe, much less yell. He squirmed, trying to get free. The one with the tattoos sat on the fender well and put his boot against Sam's cheek, pinning his head against the floor. Sam went still, and concentrated on getting enough air.

The truck turned onto a rutted dirt road, but Murdoch didn't ease off the gas. The steel floor jolted under Sam's aching body. The Indian squished him from above. And Sam was pretty sure the other guy had recently stepped in dog shit.

They traveled a mile on the bumpy road before the truck skidded to a stop in a swirling cloud of dust. Murdoch climbed out from behind the wheel while the other two dragged Sam out of the truck and dumped him in the dirt.

After the battering in the truck, the earth felt solid and comfortable. Sam sat there a few seconds, looking around. No houses in sight, no one who might help. Cottonwoods lined the narrow dirt road, their branches reaching overhead and their fallen leaves decorating the ground with yellow polka dots. The road paralleled an irrigation ditch, and the grass along the ditch was bushy and thick. Sam didn't like the looks of that rushing brown water.

"Get up," Murdoch said. He was looking around the empty pastures and alfalfa fields, checking for anyone watching. His hands were busy pulling on a pair of battered leather work gloves. Sam didn't like that, either.

He slowly clambered to his feet, feeling every previous punch and jolt in his ribcage. He didn't think he could take another working-over.

Just before he straightened all the way, he lunged forward and hit Murdoch in the gut with his shoulder. A perfect tackle, took him right off his feet. Sam was thinking that Way-Way would be proud as the other two grabbed him and pulled him away.

Murdoch got to his feet and brushed himself off, saying, "You just made it worse on yourself." His voice was flat and cold as a tombstone. "Hold him tight."

The goons obeyed, and Sam's arms went numb under the pressure.

Murdoch threw a hooking right that hit Sam in the short ribs. His breath huffed out of him, and he pitched forward, but the big men held him in place. A quick, sharp left caught him on the other side.

Then Murdoch got methodical. He punched Sam on the shoulder joint, and Sam felt the tight sinews twang under the blow. Then the other shoulder. A wicked punch to the solar plexus, which caused Sam to heave and gasp. Two to the beltline. Then back to the face until Sam passed out.

When he awoke, his head was under cold water. He choked and sputtered as he was pulled from the irrigation ditch and tossed onto the grass. Sam coughed as the three gathered around him.

The kicking commenced. Feet coming at him from every direction, hitting his knees, his ribs, his arms as he covered his face. One caught him on the temple, and Sam saw stars before welcome blackness overtook him.

28

WHEN SAM AWOKE, he was surrounded by faces staring down at him. A smiling Asian with black-rimmed glasses, wearing a dazzling white coat and a stethoscope. Sergeant Rey Delgado, looking dapper as usual. Across from them, Robin, her face etched with worry. She was wearing a dress, for Christ's sake, and holding a bouquet of flowers.

"He's coming around," Delgado said.

The smiling doctor leaned over Sam, shined a penlight in his eyes. "His pupils seem okay," he said. "But I'd bet money on a concussion."

Sam felt achy and floaty and strange. He glanced around the bed, saw the IV tube feeding into the inside of his elbow. Drugs. He frowned. Hard to tell how bad he was hurt with drugs flowing through his system. Of course, without the drugs, he might be in no shape for anything.

"How bad?" he croaked.

"You'll live," Delgado said. "Dr. Lee here says it looks like a professional job."

The doctor nodded briskly, smiling.

"They knew what they were doing," he said. "You've got bruising all over, maybe some internal injury, almost certainly a concussion. But no broken bones, probably no permanent damage."

Robin had set her flowers down somewhere, and she busied herself with pouring Sam a plastic cup full of water. He drank it through a straw, watching her. She had a look on her face, no doubt intended to be meaningful, but Sam was so dopey he couldn't decipher it.

"You look nice," he said. "New dress?"

She rolled her eyes. "This is the dress I wear to funerals."

"Am I hurt worse than I know?"

She rested a hand on his arm. "I wasn't sure when I headed over here."

"Where am I anyway?"

"University Hospital," Delgado said. "A jogger found you on the ditchbank about three hours ago. Good thing, too. If you'd been out there all night, you might've frozen to death."

Three hours. Sam let his eyes roam the white hospital room. The windows were covered with mini-blinds, but through the slits he could see it was dark outside.

"Who did this to you, Mr. Hill?" Delgado asked.

"I don't know." Sam's voice worked better now that he'd had a drink.

"Somebody worked you over, and you don't know who it was?"

"I'm drawing a blank. Maybe I do have a concussion. Could it give me amnesia, doc?"

Dr. Lee's smile winked out for a second while he thought it over, then went back to the high-beams.

"Amnesia's rare, but a blow to the head could juggle your memory for a while. And maybe the other damage was done while you were already unconscious."

Sam liked this theory, though it was dead wrong. "That must be it. I must've been out cold."

Delgado shook his head and looked toward the ceiling.

"What are you doing here, Sergeant?" Sam said. "This doesn't seem like an auto theft problem."

Delgado glanced at Robin, then smiled wryly. "Way I hear it, everything you do is an auto theft problem."

Sam tried to smile, too, but his face hurt. He was briefly glad no mirrors were nearby.

"I heard the call on the scanner, recognized your name," Delgado said. "Thought it might be connected."

"Connected to what?"

Delgado rubbed a hand over his dark face, came up grinning.

"Okay, if that's the way you want to play it," he said. "You getting beat up, that's got nothing to do with Phil Ortiz or the DEA or that Thunderbird with the corpse in it."

Sam glanced at the others. Dr. Lee waited patiently, still smiling his ass off, like nothing they could say would faze him. Robin was watching Delgado. Sam thought he saw a little too much appreciation in her eyes. The detective was handsome, sure, but he was a frigging cop. Surely, Robin wouldn't—

"Last chance," Delgado said.

"I'm a little woozy, Sergeant. Feels like my memory is getting worse."

Delgado nodded, as if that was the answer he'd expected. "Have it your way. You're right, it's not my problem. A uniform will take your statement, assuming you ever have one."

The detective stared at Sam for a few seconds, waiting, then looked up at Robin. "Guess that beating didn't soften him up any. He's still hard-headed as ever."

Robin smiled at him, and Sam didn't like the way they looked at each other.

"It would take more than a beating to change that," she said.

Delgado said goodbye to all of them, but he didn't take his eyes off Robin until he left.

As the door closed behind the detective, Sam said, "That cop the new president of your fan club?"

Robin flushed, and Sam saw he'd hit a nerve. Better not to think about what that meant. He swiveled his head to look at the patient doctor.

"Do I get to go home now?"

Dr. Lee shook his head vigorously, apparently delighted to deliver the news: "You're staying with us overnight. We need to run a few tests. I think you'll go home tomorrow. You'll have to take it easy for a few days, but you'll be fine. Like I said, this guy knew what he was doing."

The doctor still smiling to beat the band, as if he highly approved of the assailant's technique.

"Come on, doc. How do you know it was an expert job? You see that many around here?"

"I work in the trauma unit. I've seen it all. Usually, a guy like you comes in, and he's missing teeth, he's at least got a few broken fingers, a broken nose. You, on the other hand, look like you lost a boxing match. Takes a certain amount of skill to punch like that, just hard enough, without cracking ribs or anything, unless the guy was wearing boxing gloves."

Sam shook his head.

"I didn't think so." The doctor's smile broadened, though that hadn't seemed possible. "I must hurry along now. Get some rest. I'll be in to check on you in an hour or two."

The doctor fiddled with the IV, then smiled his way out the door. Sam turned to Robin, standing by his bedside. "Guy works in the trauma unit. Why's he so happy?"

"Maybe he likes trauma. Some people are into that sort of thing. You, for instance, appear to have a death wish."

"Here we go," he said. "I knew, as soon as the others left, I'd get a lecture."

"I'm not going to lecture you. When Delgado called, told me you were in the hospital, it scared the hell out of me. But lecturing won't do any good with you."

"Delgado called? Why?"

"What do you mean?"

"Why did he call you? He doesn't know us. He shouldn't care whether you find out I'm here or not."

"Maybe it was his good deed for the day."

"I think he wanted another glimpse of you, that's what. And then you show up, wearing that dress—"

"Oh, for shit's sake," she said. "Listen to you. You're jealous of a *cop*?"

"I don't have a jealous bone in my body."

"You're lucky you have *any* bones left in your body."

Sam paused. He wanted to tease her some more about Delgado, but a wave of warmth washed through his body and he had trouble concentrating. More drugs. Dr. Lee must've fed another blast into the IV on his way out the door. Sam suddenly had trouble focusing his eyes.

"Uh-oh."

"What?" Concern crimped Robin's face.

"The doctor slipped me a mickey. I'm getting sleepy."

Her expression relaxed and she patted his arm. "Want to talk to me first? Tell me what happened?"

"Ortiz's boys. Two of them held me while the other one hit me. Then they kicked me a while."

He blinked his eyes, fighting to stay awake.

"I tried to warn you, Sam. If you were smart, you would've stayed out of this. Now look at you, hurt and in the hospital."

"This sounds like that lecture I was talking about."

"You're right. I shouldn't nag. It's over now, at least."

"It's not over."

"You think you're in any shape to go after him again? Look at you. You'll be healing for weeks."

Sam said nothing, feeling the druggy lightness flow through him.

"You're conking out," she said. "I should go. Just let me give you my flowers. I bought them downstairs. Did you see them?"

She disappeared from view around the end of the bed, then appeared on the other side, holding a bouquet of dahlias and tiger lilies. The fat vase was shaped like a howling coyote, done in blacks and reds, the stems of the flowers jutting from the coyote's upturned mouth.

"Nice," Sam said. "Looks like he's puking up flowers."

"Santa Fe kitsch," she said, "but I had to get it. The coyote's perfect for you. The Indians call him the Trickster."

Sam opened his mouth to object, but a fog rolled over his brain, and his eyelids closed. He struggled against the drugs, tried to talk, tried to tell her one important thing, if only he could remember.

29

SUNLIGHT POURED INTO the hospital room when Sam next awoke. He was a little fuzzy about whether he'd been given more painkillers during the night, but they'd definitely worn off now.

He raised his aching head and looked around the bright room. Empty.

A nurse call button was clipped to his pillow and he reached for it, ready to summon more drugs, but it hurt his ribs too much to raise his arm.

Sam lifted the sheet and gingerly pulled aside the backless hospital gown he was wearing. His chest and abdomen were mottled with bruises, large enough to bleed together, so there were places where all the skin was purple and black. Jesus.

He gently flexed muscles in his scraped legs and bruised arms, trying to find someplace that didn't hurt. No luck.

He covered himself and looked around the room. His eyes came to rest on the floral arrangement Robin had brought him. The howling coyote vase. The Trickster.

She had him pegged. All his life, Sam had a fetish for practical jokes. To see others flustered and confused by some trick he'd arranged was the sweetest little thrill. That's why he couldn't pass up the gag with the T-Bird, even if it did only make matters worse with Phil Ortiz.

Ortiz. Sam wasn't done with him. He needed to get on the horn, start setting things up, but reaching the phone seemed out of the question at the moment.

Robin was right—as usual. A smart man would heal up and keep his head down and try to stay out of Ortiz's way in the future. A smart man would learn something from this beating, maybe change his ways.

But Sam had too much pride to take a whipping, then tuck his tail and slink away. Ortiz thought he was sending Sam a message, but the beating scrambled the signal. He wanted to scare Sam so badly that he would go retrieve the Our Lady of Guadalupe car. But it wasn't fear Sam felt, it was rage.

Ortiz needed to pay. It was up to Trickster Sam to make that happen. Just as soon as he could move again.

The door burst open and Way-Way squeezed through, trailing a skinny nurse who squawked about visitors' hours. The flustered nurse elbowed her way back out into the hall, screeching about calling Security. Way-Way showed no sign of noticing her.

"How you feeling, Sam?"

Way-Way loomed over the bed, seemed to blot out the ceiling. The perspective—looking right up the big man's nose—made Sam a little woozy.

"Like hell," he said. "All my painkillers wore off."

"Want me to go get you some?"

Sam imagined what that might entail, picturing cops and property damage and blood everywhere.

"No, that's okay. Just push that call button for me."

"They'll bring drugs?"

"We'll see."

Way-Way pushed the button, then looked him over and declared, "I've seen worse. But next time you play linebacker, you should wear a helmet."

"Thanks."

The door opened a foot and a short nurse poked her round face inside. She took one look at Way-Way and her head disappeared from view so fast, it was like someone popped a balloon.

"You're scaring the help."

"I didn't do anything. They create their own fear."

Sam grinned, which made his face hurt. "That's good. Philosophical. You sound like a Nike commercial."

Way-Way's mustache twitched.

"Meanwhile, you're running off the nurses who are bringing my painkillers."

Way-Way shrugged his massive shoulders. "What do you want me to do?"

"Go pull Ortiz's head off."

"You got it." Way-Way turned on his heel and headed for the door.

"No. Wait."

The big man's boulder of a head swiveled around.

"Come back. I was kidding."

Way-Way shrugged again, and returned to Sam's bedside.

"Doesn't seem like a joking matter to me," he said. "Ortiz did this to you, I *should* go pull off his head."

"Nah, that's too easy. I've got something else in mind."

Way-Way got a twinkle in his eye. "A plan?"

"Maybe, but I'm hurting too much to—"

The door swung open, and Dr. Lee entered the room. The doctor looked Way-Way up and down, and his eyes widened and his smile flickered. The squawky nurse stood guard in the doorway, her pointy chin thrust forward like a beak.

"Hi, doc," Sam said. "Glad to see you. My drugs wore off."

Dr. Lee stayed close to the wall as he sidled past Way-Way. When he reached Sam unharmed, he beamed his bright smile again. Mr. Bedside Manner.

"No more of those drugs for you," he said.

Way-Way made a growling noise.

"New drugs. Different drugs."

The doctor fished in the pocket of his white lab coat and came up with a brown prescription bottle. He rattled the pills inside.

"Percocet," he said. "These'll do the job, but you can still get up and move around."

"I can go home."

"You bet. Your, um—" The doctor glanced over at Way-Way. He came up to the big man's belt. "—*friend* here can drive you home?"

"Sure."

"You can't drive while you're taking these," the doctor said. "You should stay in bed, eat soup, ease back into your daily routine."

"Gotcha. Way I'm feeling right now, I don't have any choice. I have to take it easy."

This amused the hell out of Dr. Lee, but then most everything did. Sam squinted against the brilliance of his smile.

"All our tests were negative," the doctor said. "All you've got is superficial damage. You'll heal. But it'll take time."

Dr. Lee gave him a pill and some water, and Sam quickly swallowed it. The doctor wrote out a prescription.

"When these are all gone," he said as he handed the paper to Sam, "you'll be ready for Tylenol. Any problems, call the hospital. They'll find me."

Dr. Lee orbited Way-Way and left. The skinny nurse shot them a final glare, then closed the door.

"Glad that's over," Way-Way said. "I hate medical stuff."

"Wasn't like he opened me up here in the bed."

"Still. You know that channel on TV? The one that's always showing surgery?"

"On cable."

"I'll be flipping around the remote and I hit that channel and it's like, Jesus, that's somebody's *insides* there. It freaks me out."

"Lot of stuff freaks you out."

"There's a lot of weird shit in the world."

"You said it."

"Which brings us back to Phil Ortiz."

Sam felt the first tingly numbness from the drug. It couldn't come soon enough. He hurt so bad, he couldn't move a muscle. And he needed to pee.

"First, get me out of here," he said. "Find my clothes."

Way-Way slammed open the door to a closet built into the wall and reached in to fetch Sam's clothes. They were wadded in a clear plastic garbage bag, his black sneakers on the top.

"Nice," Sam said. "Might be a little wrinkled."

Way-Way dropped the bag on the bed. "Want me to dress you?"

"No, thanks. You might pull my arms off by accident. Just let me rest until the drug takes hold, then I'll do it and we'll get out of here."

A rustle at the door caught their attention and they looked over in time to see a thin sheaf of stapled white pages slide under the door.

"Those would be my discharge papers," Sam said.

"Under the door? What is this, the Hilton?"

"I told you, they're scared of you."

"Because I'm big."

"I think it's the expression on your face. You look like you're mad about something. You should try smiling more."

Way-Way's face creased into the familiar scowl of the irritated bouncer.

"Maybe you should grow some hair," Sam offered.

"Maybe you should bite me."

"I don't have the strength."

Way-Way pulled Sam's clothes out of the bag and started spreading them out on the foot of the bed.

"Come on. Jump into your clothes, and we'll go kill Ortiz."

"Stop saying that. The cops were here last night. They probably bugged the room."

"You think?"

Sam struggled into a sitting position, throbs rippling through his body with every movement. The Percocet was helping, though. He blinked against the pain.

"Besides, I told you, I don't want to kill Ortiz," he said, once he caught his breath. "I've got something else in mind for him."

"Yeah?"

"Something slow. I want him to suffer."

"Like you're doing now?"

"Worse."

Way-Way's bottom lip jutted out while he considered this. "Good."

"But first," Sam said, "I need to go home and recover some more. Tomorrow, we'll have a meeting. You, me, and Billy."

"You gonna let Ortiz just walk around until then?"

"Sure. I want him to think I'm out of the game. He'll get curious. He'll come around eventually, wanting to know about his stupid low-rider."

"He's still after that car?"

"That's the only reason they didn't kill me. I'm supposed to steal it back for him."

"You gonna do it?"

"You'll see."

30

THERE WAS NO QUESTION about where they'd hold the meeting on Monday afternoon. Sam could barely move from bed to his armchair in the living room without pharmaceutical assistance, but he was trying to ease off the pills. He needed to think clearly.

He'd spent much of the morning at the bathroom mirror, examining his fat lip and the two shiners that squeezed his eyes to slits. Looked like he was wearing a mask. The Lone Ranger. His chest and abdomen still were mottled, though the bruises were changing from deep purple to a greenish-brown. Healing already, but they still hurt like hell.

Sam figured it was safe for Way-Way and Billy to come to him. Delgado had seen Sam was all bunged-up, in no condition to cause further mischief. Besides, the cops were probably busy watching Phil Ortiz now.

The lock on the front door was broken, and Sam shouted for Billy and Way-Way to let themselves in so he wouldn't have to get up from his chair.

Sunshine glared on the windows, but a chill breeze rushed into the room before Billy could get the door shut. Might be cold tonight, Sam thought, which won't help all the stiffness in my muscles and joints.

Billy examined the broken door jamb, and told Sam he'd fix it for him. Then he fetched coffee all around, while Way-Way occupied the sofa, which sagged under his weight. Billy sat on a Mexican rug near Sam's feet, like a kid waiting to hear a story.

"Okay," Sam said, "here's the deal: This bastard Ortiz made a mistake. It's one thing screwing around with the cops and swapping the dead guy back and forth. That was kinda fun.

"But now it's gotten personal. Ortiz told his boys to hold me while this guy Johnny Murdoch beat the hell out of me. When they were done, he told them to take me out to the ditchbank and do it *again*."

"That's going too far," Way-Way said.

"Damned straight," said Billy.

"All right then. So what we need is a way to hurt Phil Ortiz, give him a little of what he's dishing out."

"I'll do it," Way-Way said. "Catch him alone somewhere. Work him over slowly."

"No," Sam said, "that's too easy. Use your imagination. How do we get even with Ortiz? What's the one way to really hurt him?"

Light dawned in Billy's eyes. "His cars."

"Very good, William."

Way-Way grinned. "We torch his garage?"

"Jesus, no," Billy moaned. "I couldn't destroy all those old cars."

"We won't destroy them," Sam said. "We'll *steal* them."

31

SAM SNOOZED MUCH of the way to Santa Fe that night, worn out from the planning and the phoning and the pain. Billy, behind the wheel of the Mustang, seemed to recognize that his passenger was pooped, and mostly kept his mouth shut as they sped through the hills north on I-25.

"Sam?" he said at one point, after Sam stirred next to him.

"Mm?"

"How come we didn't bring Way-Way?"

"Don't need him. This is an easy job."

"Banged up as you are, I don't see how anything's easy."

"I just need to take it slow."

"Way-Way could do the heavy work. Tearing off garage doors, stuff like that."

"He's got a job. We'll need him tomorrow, so he ought to work at The Tropics tonight."

"Still."

Way-Way had wanted to come. Talking him out of it was the second-hardest task Sam had undertaken all day. The giant had conceded only when Sam said, "I want you for the big fish. Tonight, we're just going after the bait."

The hardest job, not surprisingly, had been getting Robin to play along. She still was upset with his stubbornness, and it took a great deal of sweet talk (and playing on her sympathies by groaning over every ache) to get her to agree to help. Once she got on board, though, Robin came through like a champ. She collected the information he needed, then volunteered to handle some set-up work, arranging the "heavy equipment," as they called it over the phone.

Billy rounded up drivers for tomorrow's job and made other calls. Fetched Sam coffee and aspirin so he could keep going.

Despite all the help, Sam was exhausted. It was past eight already, and he had another couple of hours before he could get back into bed and zone out on painkillers. He could sleep late tomorrow. By the evening, he might be halfway mobile again.

Billy exited the freeway onto Old Santa Fe Trail, the lights of houses sprinkled about the black velvet of the rolling landscape. Sam leaned his head against the window and looked up at the starry sky. The moon was a curved sliver, what Bunker always called "Grandpa's toenail," and Sam found comfort in the darkness.

Streets in the capital city tend to be narrow and crooked, following old burro trails and ancient trade routes. Billy navigated them smoothly. He'd studied a map at Sam's place and memorized what they needed. The kid had a kind of native talent—he could visualize a route from a map better than anyone Sam had ever met.

The place they were seeking was up in the foothills of the Sangre de Cristo Mountains, off a winding road east of town. The dirt road got increasingly rutted and eroded the farther they crept along. Up here, it was a maxim: the more expensive the property, the worse the road leading to it. Santa Fe's version of a moat.

Many of the driveways had gates, and the houses hulked among piñon and juniper trees. Big-money people, hiding away in their adobe haciendas, buying into the Southwestern lifestyle—white wine and gallery openings and broomstick skirts and tailgate parties at the Opera.

Lot of the rich folks in Santa Fe come from California, so Sam hadn't been surprised to learn that Robin's client was a movie producer. Sam had never heard of Leonard Trumpett, but apparently the guy had seen some success in Hollywood. Billy recognized the name, said Trumpett made action movies.

"Specializes in blowing things up," he'd said.

"I thought that's what they all did in Hollywood," Sam said.

"Trumpett's movies actually made money. Still, he's better known for his wife."

"And she would be?"

"Tara Hall."

"Who?"

"You don't remember her? Blond actress, used to be on that hospital show, *Emergency Unit.*"

"I've never watched a hospital show in my life."

"She was a big deal for a while. Made a couple of movies. I haven't seen much of her lately."

"That's because they're not in Hollywood anymore. They're here in Santa Fe, dodging California taxes."

Billy braked as they reached Trumpett's address. The house sat back from the road, a few lights on, but barely noticeable among the dark dwarf forest.

"That's it," Billy said. "Looks like a barn out back."

"A barn. That's what a movie producer needs. You see any livestock?"

"Looks like there might be a corral in the back there, but I'm guessing the barn's where he keeps his cars."

"Sounds right. I'll get out here."

"Sure you don't want me to do the boost? You could drive my car back."

"Nah, I'll do it. But hang around out here, in case something goes wrong. I can't very well go sprinting off through the trees."

"I'll make a few passes up and down this road. But don't take too long. Not much traffic up here. Somebody might notice a car cruising around."

Sam popped open the door and gave Billy a look under the dome light.

"I've done this before," he said.

"Sure, Sam, I'm just saying—"

"See you in Albuquerque."

Sam got out and gently shut the door. He stepped onto the shoulder as Billy let the Mustang creep away.

Once the car was out of sight over a hill, Sam headed off through the trees, feeling his way along, shuffling under the pain that still snatched at his shoulders and ribs.

No fence running around the property. No barking dogs. Just

the trees and the night and the scent of fireplace smoke. Sam figured that swells like Trumpett counted on their alarm systems and their privileged positions to keep burglars at bay. Sam hoped the barn wasn't alarmed. He had the tools and the know-how to disable most alarm systems, but tonight he didn't have the necessary speed of movement.

No sound came from the house, but he heard the crackle and pop of tires on the gravel road. Billy, headed back the other way, keeping an eye out for him. Sam thinking: I'd better make this good. I'm going so slowly, Billy will be back home before I even make it to the barn.

The barn was a flat-roofed building with two overhead doors on one side and a corral made of steel pipes on the other. Sam didn't see any horses, but the odor of manure wafted from somewhere.

The door he wanted was in the middle of the building, a standard wooden door with four windowpanes in the upper half. He used his penlight to check the jambs for wires and the glass for alarm tape, but found nothing. He made a fist inside his leather glove and pushed out one of the lower panes. Pop, tinkle.

Sam waited a few seconds, but there was no shrieking alarm. No lights came on in the house or yard.

He reached inside and unlocked the deadbolt and let himself into the building. He shined his light around, saw a new Lexus SUV and an old pickup and an older tractor. Stacked boxes. Saddles and bridles hanging on the far wall. Sam weaved among the assembled junk and found what he was seeking behind the rusty tractor: a long car covered by a tarp.

He still couldn't get over it. Here was this Hollywood guy, worth a mint, and he gets such a boner over some low-rider that he commits a few felonies to procure it. Then the moron stashes the stolen car at his own house, where any curious cop could ruin him.

Sam had felt bad about stealing from a client, but if Trumpett was this damned stupid, he *deserved* to be a victim. He certainly didn't deserve to own a singular automobile like Our Lady of Guadalupe.

Sam clenched his teeth against his painful stiffness as he eased the tarp off the car, working by feel, bumping around in the dark. Once the canvas was peeled away, he flicked on his penlight long enough to make sure he had the right car. Green paint sparkled under the beam. On the hood, the colorful Virgin Mary, surrounded by an aura of lighter shades of green. The low-slung car was uglier than a wart, as far as Sam was concerned, but apparently Trumpett had a weakness for kitsch.

The Impala wasn't even locked. Sam slid in behind the wheel and, holding his penlight between his teeth, groaned his way under the dash to the familiar ignition wires. Within seconds, the wires sparked and the starter turned over. The engine throbbed, and he prayed it wasn't loud enough to be heard in the house.

He looked around the car, searching for a remote control, but there was none, and he was forced to get out of the Impala and find the button that would make the garage door roll up. It rose with a clatter, and Sam hurried, as best he could, to get behind the wheel and get out of there.

The low-rider shot forward, dragging its rear on the edge of the concrete as it bumped into the dirt yard.

A floodlight came on next to the back door of the house. Sam muttered a curse and stepped on the gas, the car scraping and jouncing on its hydraulic suspension.

The door flung open and a tall blond woman strode outside. She wore jeans and a loose white top and her hair was pulled back into a ponytail. Tara Hall, Sam guessed, and he stared as he passed, trying to recognize her from TV.

He was so busy gawking, he almost didn't notice that the actress had a chrome-plated pistol in her hands. She jacked the slide. Sam said, "Yikes!" and stomped the accelerator, the car shuddering as it lurched across the dirt yard toward the road.

A shot cracked in the night, and Sam pulled his shoulders up, trying to hide his head like a turtle. The low-rider's rear tires spun as he reached the road, which was higher than the yard. The rear bumper was against the ground, keeping the tires from getting purchase in the loose dirt.

Pop. Another gunshot. Sam cursed, cut the wheel and goosed the accelerator. The low-rider climbed up onto the road, fishtailing in the gravel as another shot spider-webbed the back window.

Sam drove as fast as he dared in the low car, jolting over every rut and bump. The Impala wasn't built for backcountry driving, and none of Phil Ortiz's modifications helped. The suspension was stiff and the tires were narrow and hard. The steering wheel was made of welded chrome chain, half the size it should've been, and Sam's gloves slipped as he wheeled it through curves, headed back toward town.

Headlights loomed behind him, and he made out in the mirror that it was Billy's Mustang, hard on his heels. Another set of headlights topped a rise farther back and flashed to high beams. The vehicle approached fast over the bad road, and Sam would've bet a grand that it was the SUV he'd seen in the barn.

He reached inside his jacket for his phone, ready to alert Billy, but the kid was already on it. The Mustang slowed, letting Sam run on ahead. He watched in the mirror as Billy centered his car on the road, not leaving the pursuer room to pass. The SUV honked and flashed its lights.

Sam wondered whether the actress or her husband was behind the wheel of the pursuing truck. He hoped it was Trumpett. Tara Hall had seemed a little trigger-happy.

He gunned the Impala as it reached a paved road and roared away, the rear bumper throwing sparks at every pothole.

32

IT WAS A LITTLE CLOSE inside Way-Way's van Tuesday afternoon, and somebody's deodorant had stopped working. Sam sat up front in the passenger seat, the window open, but still the stench found his nose. Way-Way, behind the wheel, didn't seem to notice. He leaned his shaved head against the back of his seat, relaxed. Everyone else in the van was strung tight with tension, but Way-Way looked ready to doze off.

Sam swiveled in the seat to look at the men sitting on the floor of the van's cargo area. The big, hairy, leather-clad biker, Bruno, who worked for Robin. A young, freckled black man called Red. An old-timer named Gus, whose nose was flattened from a lifetime of brawls. Two friends of Billy's, young guys with bad haircuts and nervous smiles; Sam hadn't caught their names. And, finally, a middle-aged guy named Fred, who made up for his thinning hair with bushy eyebrows and a droopy mustache. No one was reacting to the odor in the van, which convinced Sam that it came from Bruno. Scary as the biker looked, none of the others would dare say anything.

Quite a crew. Not bad, considering how rapidly it was assembled. Most had been eager volunteers, though Fred and Gus had taken some persuading. They'd been around long enough to know the benefits of caution. But Sam dangled free cars in front of them, and they couldn't resist.

Three others were part of the crew. Two were Robin's people—a skinny kid named Felipe and another hairy biker type called Mike—who sat behind the steering wheels of stolen flatbed tow trucks, parked behind the van. The third was Billy, who waited in Our Lady of Guadalupe.

Sam wasn't happy about Billy driving the low-rider. The kid was good behind the wheel, but there was a chance Ortiz would catch him. Sam didn't like putting Billy in that position. Nothing to be done for it, though. Nobody else was willing to take that risk, and he couldn't drive the low-rider himself. He needed to be here in the van, the leader, to keep the others on schedule.

The way Sam had it figured they'd have maybe ten minutes, depending on how long Billy could keep Ortiz occupied. Ten minutes was barely enough, even if everything went like clockwork.

The sun was low in the sky, lighting up the yellow cottonwood leaves so brightly it was almost painful to watch. Sam checked his watch. Maybe half an hour of daylight left.

"Okay, fellas," he said. "Time to roll."

Way-Way straightened up behind the wheel and cranked the engine. The others shuffled and shifted, getting ready, checking their tools and re-tying their shoes.

Sam used binoculars to take one last look at Ortiz's place. They were parked nearly a mile away, with nothing but open pastures between them and the house. If Ortiz happened to glance over here, see the wreckers and the van parked on the country road, he'd know something was up. It was important that Billy do a good job in getting Ortiz's attention turned the other direction.

No movement around the house. A sleek silver Mercedes and Johnny Murdoch's pickup were parked out front.

Sam hit the speed-dial on his cell. Billy answered on the first ring.

"You ready?" Sam asked.

"You bet."

"Just do it as we rehearsed. Soon as you're sure they're after you, haul ass back into town."

"Got it."

"Be careful, Billy."

The phone clicked dead and Sam watched as the Impala bumped out of a dirt driveway, where Billy had kept it hidden behind some evergreen shrubs, then took off for Ortiz's fortress. Billy didn't even wave. Sam saw the look of determination on the kid's sharp face, and knew he'd be fine.

He watched through the glasses as the low-rider swerved through the two curves leading up to Ortiz's place. Billy steered the car into the driveway and stopped between the two pillars where they'd left the T-Bird days before. Across the mile of pastures, Sam could hear the Impala's horn honk.

Billy laid down on the horn twice more before Ortiz and Murdoch burst out of the house, pointing and running.

"Go, Billy, go," Sam said under his breath.

On cue, the Impala swung backward into the road and zoomed off. Ortiz and Murdoch ran to the Mercedes and screeched away after the low-rider. Billy had a decent head start.

"Hit it."

Way-Way threw the van into gear and sped toward Ortiz's house. Sam checked the side mirror, making sure Felipe and Mike followed in the wreckers.

Two minutes later, Way-Way drove into Ortiz's driveway, headed toward his fancy garage. The tow trucks roared along behind them, their chains rattling.

As soon as the van jerked to a halt, Way-Way jumped out and headed for the house, as planned. If any of Ortiz's people remained behind, Way-Way would take care of them. Sam figured Ortiz was so excited about seeing Our Lady, he hadn't taken a moment to set the house's security system.

The rest of the crew piled out of the van and ran toward the garage. Sam, moving stiffly, followed. Bruno used a crowbar to pop a locked door into the garage. Probably set off all kinds of alarms, but if so, they were silent ones. By the time some rent-a-cop drove out here to check on it, Sam and friends would be long gone.

The others were eager. They raced around, pulling tarps off Ortiz's expensive hot rods. Red and Bruno whistled and cooed approvingly at the sight of the cars. Fred and Gus said nothing, efficiently going about their business.

As Sam had noticed when he was here before, keys to the cars hung on a pegboard near the washing-up sink. He passed them out.

"Fill up the wreckers first," he reminded them. "Then pick one and drive it out of here."

Red rolled up the garage doors while the others fitted keys into ignitions and kicked engines into life. Felipe and Mike had managed to turn the big tow trucks around in the driveway—no mean trick—and Sam smiled at the gouges the tires had left in Ortiz's smooth lawn.

Way-Way was behind Felipe's truck, letting down the long flatbed, turning it into a steel ramp so a car could be hauled aboard. He saw Sam looking and flashed him an "okay" sign, which meant he'd found none of Ortiz's people. So far, so good.

Fred pulled out in the first car, a late '40s Ford with rounded fenders and thudding chrome exhaust pipes. The car bumped up onto the ramp, then Fred jumped out and helped Felipe winch it into place.

Meanwhile, Gus was in another hot-rod, a chopped-and-channeled Plymouth, steering it up onto Mike's truck. Once both cars were chained in place, the drivers pushed levers and the hydraulics whined as the beds returned to horizontal positions.

Sam picked a '55 Chevy Bel Air out of the herd, and snugged it up close to the rear of Felipe's truck, so it could be hitched and pulled along behind. The tow trucks could take away two cars each. The rest would be driven away under their own power.

Felipe waved as he swung up into the cab of the wrecker. He'd left the big engine running, and now it roared as he threw it into gear.

Sam hobbled back to the garage, where Billy's two friends were arguing over an old Buick with flames painted on the hood. He'd expected something like this. "Just grab a car, goddammit. I'll take that one."

They grumbled, but obeyed. Both got behind the wheels of other cars as Bruno and Red roared out of the garage. Gus and Fred were right behind them in two others.

Three cars remained—the Buick, an old Hudson, and a blue Pontiac GTO musclecar with white racing stripes. Sam would've preferred the GTO, but he'd said he'd take the flaming Buick, so he was stuck with it. The car had a wide chrome grille and an underbite of a bumper, which made it look like a sea bass. He hated to leave the other two cars behind, but he was out of drivers. Way-Way already was behind the wheel of his old van, ready to bring up the rear.

Sam oomphed into place behind the wheel and cranked the Buick's starter. It caught right away. He revved the straight-eight engine, then threw it into gear, leaving two black stripes of burnt rubber across the concrete floor of Phil Ortiz's pristine garage.

Then he was out on the road, Way-Way's van close behind him, one of the tow trucks disappearing from sight up ahead, the other stolen cars strung out in between.

As the caravan reached Isleta Boulevard, cars peeled off in different directions, as planned. Sam didn't care where the crew took the individual cars. They were theirs to keep, as promised when they came on board. As long as they kept the cars stashed for a while, they could safely resell them for a bundle. Mike carried his two to one of Robin's chop shops—it seemed only fair that Robin profit from the boost.

Felipe's tow truck made a beeline for South Broadway. Sam and Way-Way caught up with it a few minutes later.

The wrecker slowed as it reached Morelos Automotive. The lights were out in Ernesto's office, as Sam had hoped, and the place looked locked up for the night. The wrecker stopped in the dirt parking lot, and Way-Way swung his van around it, headed for the gate into Ernesto's salvage yard.

Sam stopped in the parking lot near the road, keeping watch. Way-Way lumbered out of the van, bolt-cutters in hand, and made quick work of the lock-and-chain that kept the gate secured. He swung the ten-foot-wide gate open and Felipe drove the tow rig inside.

Felipe came running out a minute later, battery cables dangling from his hand, and ran for the van as Way-Way swung the gate closed.

Good. Sam had watched to make sure Felipe remembered to disable the stolen wrecker before they left it there. He swung the Buick up onto the road and drove away, watching his mirrors as Way-Way followed.

Only when Morelos Automotive was out of sight did Sam allow himself to relax. He took a deep breath, despite the discomfort in his ribs, and blew it out, fogging the Buick's windshield.

He dialed Mitch's Auto Salvage on his cell phone and Robin picked up on the first ring.

"Hi there," he said.

"God, I thought you'd never call. Did it go all right?"

"Perfectly. I'm driving past your place right now, headed into town. Way-Way'll drop Felipe off any second. You interested in an old Buick with flames painted on the hood?"

"Oh, sure. Nobody would notice a car like that sitting in the yard."

"I'll stash it. You might want it later. Make up for that Thunderbird you didn't get."

"I should call Lieutenant Stanton now?"

"Ernesto's got three hot vehicles sitting at his place. Stanton would want to know."

"You sure about this?"

"Make the call. About time the cops took a closer look at Ernesto's operation."

She said she'd call him later, and he hung up.

One more thing to check. Sam hit the speed-dial, and said a silent prayer while he waited for Billy to answer.

"I'm here."

"Are they still on you?"

"Hell, no. I shook 'em, just like you said. Took them through those one-way streets downtown, all those traffic lights. They're probably still driving around looking for me."

"They'll give up eventually." Now that it was over, Sam allowed himself a grin. "And Phil Ortiz will get a big surprise when he gets home."

33

THE MERCEDES HIT NINETY as Phil Ortiz raced home on the freeway, anxiety chewing at his insides.

"We shoulda kept looking," Johnny Murdoch said beside him. "Car like that should be easy to spot."

"Don't you get it?" Phil snapped. "The car was a decoy. Hill *wanted* us to chase after it."

He glanced over at Murdoch, saw the ex-boxer blink twice, trying to comprehend. God, he thought, I'm surrounded by idiots.

"That wasn't Hill behind the wheel," Murdoch said finally.

"No. I'm guessing he's back at the house. That's why we're in a hurry."

The Mercedes rocketed off the freeway onto the Isleta Boulevard exit ramp. Phil braked it enough to squeal onto the wide street, then stomped the accelerator. He needed to get home before it was too late. Something very bad was happening there.

He sped along the country roads until his house was in sight. No vehicles in the yard, no sign of Hill. But as he slalomed the Mercedes through the curves, he caught sight of the garage and his heart sank. The overhead doors were standing open.

"Shit!"

Phil screeched the car to a halt in his driveway and bailed out the door. He stumbled toward the garage, not believing what he was seeing. A car door slammed behind him and Murdoch came running, went right past Phil, his head whipping around as he looked for someone to fight.

But there was no one. Sam Hill was gone. And so were most of the classic cars.

Phil's legs turned to water and he fell to his knees, his arms outstretched in anguish. He tipped his head back and roared.

"Son of a *bitch*!"

Then Murdoch was beside him, grasping his arm, trying to pull Phil to his feet.

"Come on, boss. Get up. We'll fix this somehow. We'll get him—"

"Shut up!" Phil yanked his arm free. "How can we *fix* this? You want to tell me that? You want to tell me how we're gonna get my cars back?"

Murdoch stepped away and turned his back, as if he didn't want to see Phil in this condition.

Phil ran his hands over his face, trying to regain his composure. When he looked at the garage again, he felt heat surge through his body, his loss and grief melting into a boiling rage. He pushed himself to his feet and straightened his clothes. Swallowed the bile that had risen in his throat.

"That fuckin' Hill," he said.

Murdoch turned back to him, and his slitted eyes were wider than Phil had ever seen them. Phil knew his own face must be bright red. He could feel the blood pounding in his temples.

"I'll go get him," Murdoch volunteered. "We'll—"

"No." Phil straightened his back, stiffening with resolve. "You've done enough. You started all this, putting Armas in that trunk."

Murdoch winced.

"Go call the cops," Phil said.

"The cops? You think that's a good idea? They're—"

"Shut up and do what you're told. We have to report the theft or the insurance won't pay off. We're talking a million bucks here."

Murdoch nodded and jogged toward the house.

Phil stood staring at the nearly empty garage. Only two cars left in there. The rest were gone.

The cops wouldn't do any good. Even if he told them about Hill, they wouldn't be able to prove anything. He wouldn't tell them anyway. Sam Hill was a problem he'd solve himself. Calling the cops was mere protocol, the first step in the undoubtedly long process required to cover his losses.

The money was the least of it. Phil could make back the million in a month by adding a few extra shipments from Mexico. But all the time and effort and care that had gone into assembling his collection was something he could never recover.

He tore his gaze away from the yawning doors of the garage and stumbled toward the house.

34

IT WAS FULL DARK by the time Billy got the low-rider stowed in one of Sam's rented storage units. This one was on Second Street, three miles north of downtown.

Billy took a circuitous route to get there, as instructed. He cruised surface streets, so low in the seat he could barely see over the dash. The colorful low-rider attracted honks and waves, but in Albuquerque, he could be any other youngster out for a cruise, burning gas on a weeknight. Billy didn't cruise anymore, but he was reminded that it remained the city's favorite form of cheap entertainment. A guy might have a menial job, live in a crappy apartment, but he'd go hungry to save enough money to decorate his car and roll around town, being cool.

Sam had told Billy he'd never stored a car in this unit before, in fact had never used it for anything. Just paid the rent, keeping it on hold. The place was newer than the one on San Mateo and had lights inside the units, set on a timer so you couldn't leave them on forever and run up the utility bill.

A young couple was unloading furniture from a truck at the far end of the building, but they weren't looking Billy's way. He flicked on the light and closed the unit's door, with him and the car inside.

Billy whistled nervously through his teeth. He knew he was straying from the program. He was supposed to lock up the low-rider, walk to where he'd left his Mustang, and get the hell out of there. But he couldn't help himself. He wanted to check out the Impala. Wouldn't take but a minute.

Driving the low-rider, with its weird suspension and tiny steering wheel, wasn't much fun, but he could tell by the crisp way the car responded that it didn't have the original weakass Chevy six-cylinder under the hood. He wondered what engine Ortiz had installed.

He popped the hood latch and Our Lady rose toward the ceiling. Even with the recent use and the dusty Santa Fe roads, the engine compartment was the cleanest Billy had ever seen. Every part looked brand spanking new, with not a drop of oil or glob of grease anywhere. The engine was much bigger than stock, a V-8 with twin chrome blowers mounted on the top, looked like two big pie plates, one in front of the other. Why would someone waste such a powerful engine on a low-rider, probably never topped thirty miles per hour? He guessed it was all for show. Ortiz probably left the hood up at car shows so people could admire the shiny machinery underneath. But then why paint Our Lady of Guadalupe on the hood? If the hood's going to be open …

Shit, there's no understanding car-show crazies. They weren't about driving well. They were about *looking good*. Just the kind of ostentation Sam always warned against.

Billy reached up with gloved hands to slam the hood shut, but caught himself. Something was wrong with this picture. Why would anybody, even a car nut, have *two* air filters on a low-rider? Only racecars used two air-sucking carburetors, and a low-rider was practically the opposite of a stock racer. The whole point was going slow, so people could admire your wheels.

Billy bent over, trying to see under the air filters. The back blower sat squarely over the carb, as you'd expect, but the other was mounted on a bracket over the manifold, didn't look properly connected to anything. What the hell?

The air filter had a wing nut on the top, holding it closed, and Billy turned it with his fingers, spun it until it came free. He lifted the lid off and nearly dropped it when he saw what was inside. Not a doughnut-style air filter, but a square package, wrapped in foil and sealed with duct tape. A flat silver brick packed into the round hole.

Billy set the lid aside and dug his knife out of his pocket. He flicked open the blade and poked a little hole in the foil. Couldn't tell anything, so he stuck the knife in there, dug around a little. When he pulled it out, the blade came away covered in black gunk, looked like roofing tar.

Billy gave it a sniff. He had a pretty good idea what it was.

He put everything back like he'd found it and slammed the hood. Our Lady of Guadalupe looked up at him piously as he phoned Sam.

35

It was mid-morning Wednesday when Robin finally heard from Ernesto Morelos. The fat man blustered through the door of Mitch's Auto Salvage with his nephew in tow. Chuco, his red bandana low over his eyes, hung near the door, watching.

Ernesto put his thick hands on Robin's desk and leaned across toward her. His eyes were bleary and his white shirt was rumpled and his breath carried the stink of someone who'd been up all night.

"You stupid little bitch," he snarled.

Robin rolled backward in her chair, putting some distance between them. Usually, she wouldn't tolerate name-calling, would gladly slap a hammer against the head of anyone who called her a bitch. She wasn't scared of Ernesto, but the kid by the door worried her. He'd pulled a gun on Sam and Way-Way, and she had little doubt the punk had found a new gun since then.

"Good morning to you, too," she said, and her voice didn't betray her. She sounded calm.

"Nothing good about it," Ernesto said. "I've been dealing with cops all night, thanks to you."

"I don't know what you mean."

"You called the cops and told them I was sitting on those cars stolen from Phil Ortiz."

Robin wasn't surprised that Stanton told Ernesto she was the one who'd tipped him. His way of stirring the pot. Not that it mattered. Even someone as dumb as Ernesto would've figured it out. The theft of Ortiz's car collection had Sam's footprints all over it, and she'd played a role. Naturally, Ernesto would come to her rather than face Sam or Way-Way.

"They arrest you?" she asked.

"Not for those cars," he said. "Not even Stanton's stupid enough to believe I'd leave a stolen tow truck loaded with hot cars at my place. But they checked all the other cars in the lot."

"Found some irregularities?"

The color rose in Ernesto's face again. Robin bit her lower lip, trying not to smile.

"Enough to keep me locked up all night," he said. "I bonded out this morning and came straight here to see you."

"Why's that?"

"Because you're the one who called—"

"Just doing my civic duty, Ernesto. We can't have stolen cars sitting around the salvage yards. Gives us all a bad name."

Ernesto straightened up and cut his eyes toward his nephew. He swallowed heavily, like he was trying to clear his throat of anger, and turned back to her.

"Your boyfriend really fucked up this time," he said.

"I don't know who you mean," she said.

"That rat-bastard Sam Hill."

"He's not my boyfriend."

Ernesto clamped his gappy teeth together, and a muscle pulsed in his cheek.

"Whatever," he said tightly. "You were in on it with him. Lifting those cars from Phil Ortiz and dumping them at my place."

Robin said nothing.

"Let me tell you something, girl. You and Sam Hill may think you're cute, running around, playing your little games. But you're fucking around with death."

"You threatening my life, Ernesto?"

"Not me." He smiled. "The man you need to worry about is Ortiz. I saw him last night at the police station, and he's pissed off. He knows you and Hill are responsible."

"What's he planning to do about it?"

Ernesto, still smiling, dragged a sausage-like finger across his throat.

"Your boyfriend fucked around with the wrong man this time," he said. "Ortiz will have his nuts hanging over his fireplace."

Robin made a face. "Thanks for that vivid imagery."

Ernesto showed his big teeth. Looked like he wanted to say something more, but he swallowed it and hitched up his pants and went out the door into the November sunshine, Chuco on his heels.

36

SAM HILL WASN'T SURPRISED when his doorbell rang late Wednesday morning. He was expecting company. Johnny Murdoch and his boys. Maybe Phil Ortiz himself. Ernesto Morelos and his nephew. Other Fourteenth Streeters under Chuco's command. At the very least, Lieutenant Stanton and Rey Delgado and the rest of the Auto Theft squad.

But when Sam peeked out the window beside his front door, he found "none of the above." Drug Enforcement Adminstration agents Quincy Brock and Rhetta Jones, both wearing neat suits and edgy expressions.

Sam had a pistol in his hand, ready for the worst. He tucked it under the cushion of the nearest chair and answered the door.

"The DEA," he said. "What a nice surprise."

"Can the sarcasm," Brock said. "We need to talk to you."

"Come on in."

Sam turned and shuffled back into the living room toward his usual armchair.

"You're not moving around so well," Jones said behind him.

"Getting old," Sam said as he turned to smile at her.

"That what happened to your face, too?" she said. "Old age? We heard somebody put you in the hospital."

"Word gets around," Sam said, gesturing them onto the couch.

"We hear," Jones continued, "that you couldn't—or wouldn't—identify the assailants."

Sam shrugged, which set a little tremor of pain quaking across his shoulders. He'd taken more Tylenol after Robin called and told him about Ernesto's visit to her garage, but it didn't seem to have done much good. He'd been tempted to pop another Percocet, but now was glad he hadn't. He needed his wits about him.

"We tried to warn you," Brock said. "Ortiz is dangerous."

"Yet I maintain I don't know the man."

Brock smiled thinly. "He certainly knows you. If he wasn't angry enough already, yesterday's little stunt is sure to make him crazy mad."

Sam gave them an impassive look. "Stunt?"

Brock rolled his eyes and sighed.

"Mr. Ortiz's car collection was stolen," Jones said. "As if you didn't know."

"Really? Gee, that's too bad."

"Cute," Brock said flatly. "I'd ask how you managed to steal all those cars, but you'd just deny it."

Sam nodded.

"Frankly, I don't give a shit about the cars," Brock said. "Anything bad that happens to Phil Ortiz, he deserves it. But Lieutenant Stanton at APD doesn't see it that way. He knows you did it, and he'd *love* to pin all those thefts on you."

"Then why are you here instead of him?"

"Because we made him lay off," Brock said. "He was gung-ho, ready to come over here and arrest your ass, but we told him to wait."

"Why'd you do that?" Sam had a feeling he already knew the answer.

The agents looked at each other, and Jones picked up the thread.

"Because we still want your help," she said. "We hear Ortiz may have another shipment coming in."

Sam shook his head. "We've been over this already. I won't be your snitch."

"Don't you want to get even with Ortiz?" Brock asked. "The man has you beaten up, and you don't want payback?"

Sam said nothing.

"Maybe you think you got your payback last night, stealing those cars and dumping some of them at Ernesto Morelos' place."

"Ernesto who?"

"Cute again. If you were trying to get the local cops to pursue

Morelos, you succeeded. They're all over that guy now. But if you were trying to get Ortiz's attention, you played it wrong. He'll be gunning for you now."

"Good thing you guys are here then," Sam said. "Sounds like I need police protection."

"You need it all right," Jones said. "And we can give it to you, if you help us apprehend Ortiz."

"I told you already—"

"You told us," Brock said brusquely. "But let me tell you something, buddy. If we don't get Ortiz off the street, your days are numbered. Your best bet would be to help us."

Sam stood up and creakily moved around the room. He thought better on his feet.

"Let me see if I've got this straight," he said. "First, you've got a dead informant on your hands. You try to get me to catch Ortiz for you, then threaten to charge me with murder if I don't play along. Now, you come here, telling me the only way I can stay alive is to play ball with you."

"We could still put you in that Thunderbird," Brock said.

"You know I didn't kill anybody."

"So what? We press charges, and you sit in the cooler a long time before the case gets tossed out. Or, we just turn Stanton loose. He's dying to arrest you."

"If I'm in jail," Sam said, "how can I help you nab Ortiz?"

Jones said, "You already said you won't—"

"That's right. I'm not a rat. I'm not wearing a wire for you. But let's say somebody's out there, keeping Ortiz worked up. Isn't it more likely he'll make a mistake? Or, that he'll call off whatever shipments he's got coming because he knows you guys are watching him?"

The agents swapped a look again. Sam guessed they'd had this same discussion on the way to his place. He relaxed a little. He wasn't going to jail. Not today. Not as long as Brock and Jones thought he might do some good. And if Ortiz killed him in the process? Sam didn't think there'd be a lot of mourning down at the DEA.

"What we want is evidence," Brock said. "You've been inside the man's house, his garage. Did you see anything—"

"Who says I've been in his house? I told you, I don't know the man."

Brock growled. Jones' hand flashed out, touched his arm.

"That's a neat trick, the way you make him calm down," Sam said. "Can you make him roll over, too?"

"Goddammit," Brock said as he got to his feet. "This is getting us nowhere."

Jones stood, too, saying, "We consider this your last chance, Mr. Hill. You cooperate with us, or we turn APD loose on those car thefts. Lieutenant Stanton should have no trouble making a case against you, and he won't cut you a deal."

They watched him, waiting. Sam thought about the heroin Billy had found in the low-rider. Was there some way to hand it over to these agents and still walk away?

"I'll have to think it over, make some calls," Sam said. "How much time do I have?"

"How does twenty-four hours sound?" Jones said. "We'll call tomorrow, and you tell us your decision. If it's the wrong answer, Stanton takes over."

Sam nodded. "Okay. Call me tomorrow."

"We'll do that," she said.

Brock muttered, "Hope you stay alive that long."

37

ERNESTO MORELOS SAT BEHIND his cluttered desk, all alone at his garage. Chuco had gone to meet his punk friends for lunch, and Ernesto had told his crew to take the day off. If he couldn't figure a way out of this mess with the cops, he might be firing the whole lot of them. Be paying a team of attorneys instead.

That bastard Sam Hill. Hadn't he done enough? Nearly killed old Moe, throwing a monkey wrench into the cogs of Ernesto's business. And that goon Way-Way sent three body men to the hospital. Ernesto couldn't wait to see their medical bills.

He'd known all along that it was dangerous, helping Phil Ortiz set up the car thief. Always the chance it could come back on him, the broker. But what choice did he have? You don't say no to Phil Ortiz.

Now that he'd stolen Ortiz's car collection, it was a sure bet Hill would be killed. But it would be too late to solve Ernesto's problems. Once Lieutenant Stanton started breathing down your neck, your business was screwed.

A lump of sand welled up in Ernesto's throat, and his eyes felt hot with tears. He buried his face in his hands. Goddammit. To be reduced to this, a weeping old man. All because Sam Hill thinks he's a comedian.

The bell over the door jingled, and Ernesto quickly wiped at his eyes before looking up. What he saw made him want to cry some more.

Phil Ortiz sauntered into the office, trailed by a short redheaded man with the wide, sloping shoulders of a boxer. Oh, Jesus.

Ernesto tried smiling, but his face seemed to be beyond his control. "Phil! I was just gonna call you."

"Yeah?" Ortiz stopped in front of the desk. He was dressed in a silk shirt and sleek black pants. His hair was slicked back, looked damp, like maybe he was fresh from a shower. But the dark circles under his eyes were reminders that he'd been up much of the night, too, talking to cops. "What were you going to tell me?"

"Just, you know, that I'm sorry about all this. That fucker Sam Hill. I can't believe—"

"Shut up, Ernesto."

Ernesto snapped his mouth closed.

Ortiz wandered around the office, looking over the messy desktops and the floor gritty with windblown sand. His lip curled. The redhead stayed by the front door, glancing over his shoulder to check out the parking lot. Ernesto said a quick, silent prayer that a customer, or Chuco, *somebody*, would drive up. Provide a witness, maybe keep Ortiz from killing him where he sat. But his prayers, as usual, went unanswered.

Ortiz finished his tour, ending up back across the desk from Ernesto.

"I never should've done business with you," he said. "Look at this place. Clutter's a sign of a disorganized mind. I should've known, just looking around, that you were stupid."

Ernesto sat silent, his hands clutched together on his desktop.

"This whole thing's gone to shit," Ortiz continued. "I try to get one car back and end up losing a dozen."

Ortiz paused, and Ernesto felt compelled to say something.

"You know I had nothing to do with that, Mr. Ortiz. Those cars that showed up here, I'd never seen them before. Hill must've—"

"Shut up. I know what happened. Hill put them here to get you in trouble. Having his revenge on us all. But he doesn't know the meaning of revenge. Yet."

Ernesto glanced at the redhead hanging by the door. Amusement danced in the man's narrow eyes, as if he were looking forward to taking out Sam Hill. Or maybe Ernesto himself, right away. He tried praying some more.

"I probably should pop you right now," Ortiz said. "Just for making a pig's breakfast of this situation."

Ernesto could feel his heart pounding in his chest.

"But I'm not ready to give up on you yet." Ortiz gave him a tight smile. "You might still be useful."

"Sure, Phil," Ernesto said quickly. "I'd do anything—"

Ortiz raised a manicured finger, and Ernesto remembered to shut his trap.

"Because of your incompetence, the cops are all over me," Ortiz said. "I try to pick up that fucking thief, give him what he deserves, and they'll know it for sure."

Ernesto nodded vigorously. Stanton and his people, the DEA, shit, probably the FBI, were watching all of them. But did any of these cops show up now, when he needed rescuing? Of course not.

"So here's what you're going to do," Ortiz said. "Go get Sam Hill and bring him to me. Maybe, if you do a good job, I won't kill you."

Ernesto felt his scratchy eyes widen and he blinked furiously.

"How am I gonna do that? Hill knows we're gunning for him. And, like you said, the cops are all over this thing. I try to roust him—"

Ortiz silenced him by shaking his head.

"You're not listening, Morelos. You do this thing for me, maybe I let you live. You refuse, and you're a dead man. You screw it up, and you're dead. Doesn't matter to me. I'll get Hill eventually. But it should matter a great deal to you."

Ernesto nodded. He'd like to get even with Sam Hill himself, but like this? A risky proposition right now, when Stanton was looking for a reason to lock Ernesto up forever. But did he have a choice?

"Yes, sir. I'll figure out a way. I'll get my nephew—"

"Don't tell me the details," Ortiz said. "I don't want to know. You call and tell me Sam Hill's ready for a 'meeting' with me. I'll tell you where to deliver him."

Ernesto said nothing, his brain buzzing, trying to sort out a way to accomplish what Ortiz asked.

"Do we understand each other?"

"Yes, sir. How soon you need this done?"

"Soon. Today, tomorrow. Any longer than that, and I'll consider you a failure. Show me you can do something right. For a change."

38

DARKNESS HAD FALLEN and an icy wind was kicking up dust by the time Robin called it a day. She was the last one on the premises at Mitch's Auto Salvage. Her crew had been gone more than an hour, but Robin still was catching up on the paperwork that had accumulated while she was helping Sam.

She frowned at the thought of Sam running around town, tweaking this mystery man, Phil Ortiz. She was certain he was digging himself deeper into trouble, but there seemed to be damned little she could do to stop him. Once Sam got a bug up his butt, he was relentless.

Of course, she was partly to blame. She'd helped him set up the boost of Ortiz's car collection, and she certainly stood to profit from the cars she had stashed away. Maybe if she'd put her foot down, told him no, he would've thought twice about going up against the drug dealer. But she had trouble saying no to Sam. Sometimes, she thought her feelings for him, her helplessnesss to end his mischievous ways, were the only reasons she still messed around with hot cars at all.

Robin knew she was dancing close to the edge. With Stanton after Sam, it was only a matter of time before someone made a mistake and she'd go down with him. She needed to get out of the stolen car business, focus on the Internet sales, make something legitimate of the inheritance Mitch left her. But Sam was always there, daring her to keep dancing.

She checked the bays to make sure the overhead doors were locked, then let herself out the office door, standing under the naked yellow light bulb as she locked up.

From behind her, she heard the shuffle of feet on asphalt, closing quickly. She dropped her keys and whirled just as hands snatched at her from either side, grabbing her arms. She twisted and squirmed, trying to pull away.

The men were unfamiliar—young toughs in baggy pants and flannel shirts. Robin kicked one of them in the shin with her steel-toed boot and yanked away from his grip. She spun into the other's arms, bringing her elbow up, catching him in the jaw. His head jerked to the side, but he hung onto her.

The first guy swung his fist, caught her on the forehead, and Robin saw stars as her head snapped back.

Then they both were on her. They pinned her arms behind her back and dragged her toward a big car parked in the shadow of the building.

The car was a Lincoln, and she thought she recognized the dark sedan as the trunk lid glided open, light spilling out the back.

Robin struggled, but it was no good. She screamed, but one of them clapped a hand over her mouth as they lifted her up. She looked around wildly, but there was no one. Nothing but empty blacktop, stretching away along South Broadway as far as she could see.

She got a glimpse of the man behind the wheel as he leaned out to watch the others stuff her into the trunk. He wasn't much more than a kid, but we wore a red bandana low over his cold eyes. Chuco.

Robin thinking: Chuco, you son of a bitch. I'll get you—

Then, wham, she hit the floor of the trunk and, whomp, the lid closed on her, blocking out the night.

39

SAM AND WAY-WAY ate dinner at The Tropics, the rattan fans stirring the air above their table, the noise of drunken revelers providing a backbeat to island music that spewed from speakers hidden along the walls.

Way-Way wore his work uniform—jeans and a loud Hawaiian shirt done in yellow and orange. His meal was a Caribbean dish that centered on plantains, and Sam could barely stand to look at it. He found the idea of crunchy bananas disturbing. He ate an overcooked burger and fries, washing it down with slugs of Dos Equis. Passers-by stared at them—Sam's battered face, the behemoth that was Way-Way—but Sam tried to ignore them. He had plenty on his mind already.

Keeping his voice low, he told Way-Way about Billy finding the black tar heroin stashed in the low-rider.

"So that's why Ortiz is so hot to get that Impala back," Way-Way said.

"And here we all thought he was just a car nut."

"He was using the car as a drop?"

"Apparently."

"Seems pretty public, leaving it at a car show."

"Maybe the stash was just there a little while. Say somebody was supposed to pick it up during the night, take it north to Chimayo or something. I just happened to take the car before the transaction could be completed."

"How much is that stuff worth?"

"Wholesales for fifteen hundred an ounce, and there must be ten pounds there. That's two hundred and forty thousand dollars."

Way-Way squinted at him.

"I did the math already," Sam said impatiently. "Even if the price estimate is off, it's still a shitpile of money."

Way-Way thought it over. "This movie guy, he was sitting on a small fortune in heroin the whole time and didn't know it?"

"Guy just had the car stolen, then stuck it under a tarp in his barn. Probably never even drove it anywhere for fear he'd get caught."

"Moron."

"Exactly."

"What are you gonna do with the stash?"

"I don't know yet. The DEA came to see me again this morning. They keep talking about a shipment coming in. I don't think it's this batch. I boosted that car a month ago. But it does explain why Ortiz won't let this thing go."

Way-Way pushed another shovelful of food into his mouth and said around it, "What did the DEA want?"

"They're still after me to set up Ortiz. Gave me twenty-four hours to think about it."

Way-Way's eyebrows rose. "Have you?"

"Took a nap all afternoon," Sam said.

The eyebrows again.

"I'm still healing up. I need my rest. But you haven't heard all of it."

Sam looked around the nightclub, but no one was in earshot. He told Way-Way about Ernesto's angry visit to Robin and Stanton going crazy over the car thefts and the DEA reining him in, temporarily.

"Damn," Way-Way said when he was done. "This thing's getting out of hand."

"It keeps escalating. Now we need a way to end it."

"We need to take Ortiz out of circulation."

"Or get the cops to do it for us."

"Be more fun," Way-Way said, "to get rid of him ourselves."

"But that wouldn't get Stanton off my neck. And the DEA wouldn't be happy. They need to bust Ortiz."

"If he just disappeared, the cops are all over you again?"

"Stanton, for sure. But if we found a way to hand Ortiz over to the DEA, then they might—*might*—keep their promise and make Stanton go away."

A hula girl stopped by to see if they needed new drinks. Way-Way drained the papaya juice from his coconut-shaped glass and handed it over, and she went away.

"So what we need," the big man said, "is to give that heroin back to Ortiz, then tell the cops he's got it."

"That's what I'm thinking. Give them a reason to get him off the street. Still wouldn't nail him for that informant's murder, but I've got an idea about that, too."

Sam's phone chirped, and he fished it out of his pocket and said hello.

"Sam Hill?"

A man's voice with a Spanish lilt. Sam didn't recognize it right away.

"Yeah?"

"Do you know who this is?"

Then Sam identified the voice. Ernesto Morelos, that fat fuck. How did he get this number?

"What do you want?"

"I've got a score to settle with you."

Sam looked up, met his dinner partner's eyes. Way-Way scowled at the interruption of their meal.

"What's the matter, Ernesto? The cops give you a hard time?"

"The cops are the least of the problem. I've got somebody who wants to talk to you."

"Ortiz?"

"He wants a meeting. Time for you to pay the piper, smartass."

Sam shot a look at Way-Way. The color was rising in the big man's face, as if he could hear Ernesto's end of the conversation.

"I'm not interested in a meeting," Sam said. "Ortiz wants a showdown, he can call me himself."

Way-Way nodded, savoring the idea of finally facing down Ortiz.

"Maybe you'd be more interested," Ernesto said, and Sam didn't like the sudden amusement in the sleazebag's voice, "if a friend of yours was in trouble."

Sam hesitated. "A friend of mine? Like who?"

"Robin Mitchell? She's your good friend, right?"

Without thinking, Sam scooted his chair back from the table, ready to move.

"What about Robin?"

"Let's say she's my guest."

"If anything happens to her—"

"Relax, *amigo*. Nothing bad has happened. But Chuco and his friends, they like her. They want to get to know her better."

"You let that mongrel touch her—"

"Take it easy. You agree to the meeting, and she goes home. Nothing happens."

"Where is she?"

"I have her safe and sound. I'm at my garage. You should come right away. I don't know how much longer I can keep Chuco in line."

"You son of a bitch, I'll kill—"

But Ernesto had hung up.

40

WITHIN MINUTES SAM was racing down South Broadway in the Caprice, Way-Way in the passenger seat. The giant's muscles were so tense, Sam could practically hear them humming.

"How do we know he's really got her?" Way-Way asked.

Sam used his cell phone to speed-dial Robin's home number and her business phone, but there was no answer either place. By the time he put the phone away, Mitch's Auto Salvage was in sight up ahead. The dark building looked empty.

The car rocketed up to the front door of the garage, tires squealing as Sam braked to a stop. Way-Way jumped out and ran through Sam's headlight beams and cupped his hands around his eyes to peer in the office's dark windows. He turned away, shook his head at Sam, started back for the car. Then he stopped and moved his big feet, looking at the ground.

He bent over and snatched something off the pavement, held it up for Sam to see. A ring of shiny keys.

As Way-Way got back into the car, he said, "These Robin's?"

"Gotta be," Sam said. "They must've snatched her as she was locking up."

Way-Way tightened his fist around the keyring. "That means they haven't had her long."

"I hope you're right."

Sam wheeled the car around and floored it. They'd be at Ernesto's in minutes.

"If that bastard's hurt her," Way-Way said, "I'll tear off his head and shit down his neck."

"Stay calm," Sam said, though he didn't feel calm himself. "She's all right. We just need to get her out of there."

"And how do we do that? You got guns?"

"No. They're at home."

"A plan?"

"No."

"Then what the hell—"

"I've got you, big guy. They won't be expecting that."

Sam stopped the car on the wide gravel shoulder of the road. Morelos Automotive sat up ahead, its lights ablaze.

"Get out," Sam said. "Go around and come in through the salvage yard."

"You're gonna walk right in the front door?"

"Sure."

"They might kill you before I get there."

"Nah, he wants to hand me over to Ortiz. They might rough me up a little."

"Good." Way-Way smiled as he got out of the car. "Make a lot of noise so they don't hear me coming."

Way-Way circled behind the car and loped away into the night. The Caprice leaped forward as Sam drove to Ernesto's dusty parking lot.

He got out of the car cautiously, watching the windows of Ernesto's office. He could see the fat man sitting behind his desk and a couple of Chuco's boys standing around, waiting. They dressed just like Chuco and carried the same load of surly attitude. Probably armed to the teeth.

Sam's heart pounded as he walked up to the office door. As his hand touched the doorknob, a voice came from the darkness at his left.

"Freeze, *pendejo*. Hands up."

Sam did as he was told. Chuco stepped from the shadows, a pistol raised to shoulder height, pointed at Sam's face. Chuco gave a shout, and his two boys came outside, grinning. They roughly patted Sam down, found the screwdriver and the flashlight inside his jacket. They pocketed the tools and turned to Chuco.

"He's clean," the larger of the two said.

Sam saw an opening, both the stupid shits looking at their leader. He could grab for Chuco's gun, wheel on them. But that wouldn't help Robin.

They shoved him through the office door. Sam tripped over the threshold, but caught himself before he went tumbling. He stopped in front of Ernesto's desk, the gangbangers crowding behind him.

Ernesto wore a limp white shirt, and he had his hands laced together over his bulging gut. Looked pleased with himself.

"Hello, scumbag," Sam said.

One of Chuco's boys whammed him across the back of the neck with a forearm. His head wobbled, and the room seemed to tilt. Then the world righted, and Sam could see Ernesto sitting across from him, a big, happy grin on his face.

"You always had a big mouth, Hill," he said. "Maybe we can teach you to keep it shut."

"I doubt it."

A sharp kick caught him in the back of the knee, and Sam nearly went down. That was no good. He needed to be on his feet, ready when Way-Way arrived.

He grasped the edge of Ernesto's desk and used it to hold himself upright. His knee throbbed, but he'd hurt in so many places lately, it was just one more pain to inventory.

"What happened to you?" Ernesto said. "You look like a raccoon."

"Your buddy Ortiz," Sam said. "But he didn't kill me when he had the chance."

Ernest smiled wider. "Maybe next time."

"Where's Robin?"

"Your girlfriend?" Ernesto's malevolent smiled widened. "She's around."

"You said you'd let her go."

Ernesto rocked forward in his chair and thrust a thick finger toward Sam's face. The smile had vanished.

"You don't get to say! You got nothing now. We've got you, and there will be no bargaining."

Sam's jaw clenched, and he muttered, "I knew you'd lie."

A punch thudded into his kidney, and he arched his back against the sudden pain. He'd be pissing blood for days. But first he'd make Ernesto pay for this abuse.

"A man of honor," Sam said tightly, "keeps his word."

He braced for another blow, but none came this time. He glanced over his shoulder. Chuco's two friends stood close by, ready to unleash on him again. Chuco leaned against the front door, the gun carelessly loose in his hand, a smug smile on his face. Bastard.

"You got a code of honor to live by, eh?" Ernesto said. "This code, what does it say about stealing cars?"

Sam remained silent. Ernesto wanted to talk, let him. Every minute that passed brought Way-Way that much closer.

"You've made a mistake this time, Sam Hill. You screw around with me, think you can get away with it, okay, that's one thing. But you pissed off Phil Ortiz. To him, that is—"

Ernesto spread his fat fingers wide, searching for the word, like it would fall from the sky into his hands.

"—unforgivable."

He smiled again, happy to have made his point. Still, Sam said nothing. One of the ruffians behind him gave him a shove, but he ignored it, kept his gaze fixed on Ernesto.

Ernesto held the stare for a long moment, then ran a hand over his wide forehead, wiping away glistening sweat.

"Phil Ortiz is unhappy with me, too," he said. "Because of you. But I can make him happy again. I'll hand you over to him, let him get even. Your death will be painful and slow."

Sam didn't know what Ernesto expected. Did he want him to beg? To whimper? To fight back? Any move Sam made would give the gangbangers more reason to hurt him. But if he stood mute, Ernesto eventually would get tired of the sound of his own voice. Sam didn't want to think about what would happen then.

A sound came from the garage work bays. The crash of a broken window, the clatter of shattered glass hitting the concrete floor.

"The fuck was that?" Ernesto said. "Chuco, go check that out."

Sam looked over his shoulder at Chuco, hoping he'd obey his uncle. Way-Way waited somewhere in the dark. If Chuco took his gun out there after him ...

Chuco shook his head. "I'm watching this asshole. Jorge, go see what that was."

The larger of the two bangers' eyes widened, but he caught himself and nodded. He peered through the glass of the door that opened into the garage, then turned the knob and stepped into the work area, his head whipping around as he searched the darkness for the source of the noise.

Sam got a whiff of car paint and grease from the garage before the door swung closed behind Jorge. Chuco stepped closer to the connecting door, keeping an eye on his soldier. He hit a switch beside the door, and the work bays flooded with light. Sam watched past Chuco's head, expecting to see Way-Way in there, rending Jorge into individual parts. But Jorge was alone in the garage. A couple of cars sat around in various states of undress. The kid didn't go search among them. He shrugged and came back into the office.

"Nobody there," he said.

"What made that noise?"

"I dunno."

Ernesto struggled up out of his chair. "Sounded like a broken window. And it didn't break by itself."

As he reached the connecting door, its window suddenly was filled with a mass of Hawaiian shirt. The door banged open, knocking Ernesto off his feet, and Way-Way flooded into the room.

The rest took less than ten seconds, though time seemed to slow. Sam felt as if he could see and hear and feel everything at once. Ernesto sliding across the floor on his fat butt. Chuco swinging the pistol toward Way-Way as the big man backhanded Jorge, who flew backward over a desk. The other kid crying out and digging at his pants, trying to find his gun.

Sam lunged and hit Chuco's wrist just as the pistol barked. The bullet pocked into the wall a foot above Way-Way's head.

A growl erupted from Way-Way and his big fist cuffed Chuco across the brow. The kid stumbled backward, his bandana over one eye. Sam snatched at his gun hand and another bullet ripped into the floor.

"I got him," Sam yelled. He grabbed Chuco's thin arm with both hands, then swung a knee into the kid's midsection. Foul air huffed out of Chuco as he folded over the blow. Sam twisted the pistol out of his hand, then hit Chuco across the cheek with the gun butt before the little bastard could recover.

He wheeled to train the pistol on the third gangbanger, but Way-Way already had a handful of the youth's shirt. He lifted the kid until his feet weren't touching the floor, then head-butted him. The kid's head snapped back, blood exploded from his nose, and only the whites of eyes showed. Way-Way tossed him aside like a sack of garbage.

Jorge was picking himself up off the floor, and Way-Way helped him out. He reached over the desk, got hold of Jorge's slick black hair and dragged him across the desk. Papers and pencils scattered and a phone clanged onto the floor.

Way-Way hit Jorge with his free hand, two punches so concussive Sam would swear later he could feel the impact himself. Jorge's face caved in. Way-Way threw him to one side and wheeled, ready for whoever was next.

Chuco still bent over, holding his gut. Ernesto sat on the floor, his bleary eyes wide and his mouth hanging open.

The punk tried to straighten up, and Way-Way took a step toward him. Sam said, "Let me." He shot the kid through the kneecap.

Chuco howled and fell to the floor, clawing at his gushing knee, as if he could pluck the hot bullet out of there with his bare hands. Sam ignored him. Chuco was through.

Sam turned the pistol on Ernesto, who still sat at his feet. A dark stain spread across the fat man's pants.

Way-Way's shaved head snapped around as he looked for someone else to hurt. But Chuco was busy with his wounded leg, and his two friends were unconscious. Way-Way's shoulders relaxed and he sighed.

"That was quick," he said, sounding disappointed.

"Not quick enough," Sam said. "They were working me over. Where were you?"

"Had to take the long way around. The whole yard's fenced with razor wire. Some things even I don't mess with."

"And in the garage?"

"Came in through a window in the back," Way-Way said. "Hid behind one of those cars until I caught my breath."

Sam nodded, and turned back to Ernesto. "Where's Robin?"

"I, I, I—"

Sam squatted down to face him. "What's the matter, Ernesto? Cat got your tongue? You had plenty to say a minute ago."

Ernesto couldn't take his eyes off Way-Way, who towered over the two of them. Sam slapped his fat cheek to get his attention.

"Where is she?"

"My car. In the trunk."

"That Lincoln parked around the corner?" Way-Way asked.

Ernesto nodded so vigorously his jowls jiggled.

"Gimme the keys."

Ernesto struggled to get a hand into his pocket, but his big gut was in the way. Way-Way stepped around Sam, grabbed Ernesto's collar, and yanked him to his feet.

Ernesto managed to get the keys from his pocket and hand them over. Way-Way made a face when he took them.

"They're wet."

"Ernesto pissed himself."

Way-Way glowered at the fat man.

"Come on," Sam said. "Let's go get her."

He gave Ernesto a shove, got him moving toward the door. Ernesto stepped wide to avoid his nephew, who still thrashed on the floor, crying and cursing in Spanish. Way-Way nonchalantly kicked Chuco in the chin as he passed, and the kid didn't make another sound.

Ernesto walked stiffly out into the chill wind, Sam pushing him along, keeping the gun pointed at his back. Way-Way led the way, never looking back at the havoc he left behind.

Around the corner of the concrete-block garage, Ernesto's black Lincoln sat in shadow, practically invisible. Way-Way fumbled around in the dark, trying to unlock the trunk. Muffled shouts came from inside, and Sam yelled, "Hang on, Robin."

The lid popped open and light spilled out of the trunk. Robin sat up inside, blinking and looking around.

She smiled when her eyes lit on Sam, and said, "Thought you guys would never get here."

41

ONCE THEY LOCKED ERNESTO in his own trunk, they hurried to the Caprice. Pain rippled through Sam's back as he gingerly slid under the wheel.

"You still need that gun?" Robin asked as she squeezed into the front seat between the two men.

"Forgot I had it," Sam said. He handed the pistol across the car to Way-Way. "Want to wipe the prints off that?"

Way-Way slid the clip out of the pistol and used the tail of his shirt to wipe it down as the Caprice sped north on Broadway.

"Out the window?" he asked.

"Along here anywhere will be fine," Sam said.

Way-Way cranked down the window and hurled Chuco's pistol into the cold night.

"That's better," Robin said. "Makes me nervous, you two goofs having a gun."

"'Goofs?' Is that any way to talk after we came to your rescue?"

"Weren't for you, I wouldn't have been in the trunk in the first place."

Sam had no answer for that.

"Yeah," Way-Way said. "And you owe me one shirt. I ripped mine coming through that window."

He tried to swivel in the seat to show his torn right sleeve, but there wasn't room without crushing Robin.

"How did you even know where I was?" she asked.

"Ernesto tried to use you as bait. Once Way-Way wiped out his crew, Ernesto told us you were in the trunk."

"Glad it worked. It was getting stuffy in there."

"Now Ernesto's finding out what it's like."

"Not for long," she said. "Chuco will let him out."

"I don't know. When we left, Chuco was busy bleeding. And his two friends were comatose."

"Good," she said. "Rat bastards."

"I love it when women talk that way," Way-Way said.

"Where are we going now?" she asked Sam.

"Taking you home where it's safe."

"There's more trouble coming? Sounds like you two turned the lights out at Ernesto's."

"Ortiz ordered Ernesto to bring me to him," Sam said. "He'll come hunting me."

Robin's shoulder pressed against Sam as she leaned over to give Way-Way more room. Gave him a warm feeling.

"Will that guy never go away?" she said next to his ear.

Sam shot Way-Way a look over Robin's head. The big man was smiling.

"We think we've got a way to get rid of him," Sam said.

Way-Way laughed. "Yeah, we got a *plan*."

"Do I want to hear about this?" Robin said. "Every time you get a plan, somebody gets in deeper trouble."

"Not this time," Sam said. "It's a good plan."

"What are you going to do?"

"We're giving Our Lady of Guadalupe back to Ortiz."

Robin sat bolt upright and said, "*What*?"

42

THE SIGHT OF HER WELL-LIT apartment building near downtown made Robin happy. There'd been a few minutes there, outside her office, when she wasn't sure she'd ever see it again.

Robin had her doubts about Sam's "plan." Ortiz already was tricked with the low-rider once. No way he'd fall for it again. But she tried not to think about what might happen next. Better to enjoy getting home alive.

They all piled out of the car, and Sam walked her to the door of the ground-floor apartment. Robin noted that Way-Way hung back by Sam's car, giving them room, and it reminded her of double dates in high school, the way one couple turns a blind eye to the other, everybody seeking privacy.

"Your friend's waiting," she said as they reached the door.

"He doesn't mind," Sam said. "He finds us *amusing*."

"Way-Way finds most everything amusing, doesn't he?"

"Hard to tell. He's got some kind of inner life going, but it's hidden behind all those muscles and that scowl."

"Occupational hazard," she said.

"I suppose."

Sam hesitated, seemed unsure what to say next. Robin bit her lip to keeping from laughing at his anxiety. She couldn't help herself; she had to tease him.

"Ernesto kept calling you my boyfriend."

Sam's face flushed, looked orange under the yellow porch light.

"Maybe," he said, "Ernesto isn't as dumb as he looks."

Robin felt a little flutter inside her chest. She put her hands on her hips and cocked her head to the side, studying him.

"You interested in being my boyfriend, Sam?"

His face flushed redder, and he glanced toward his car. She looked, too, saw that Way-Way had turned his back to them, making a show of looking out at the street. What a couple of *boys*.

"I've been having thoughts along those lines," Sam said. "But it's complicated, with business and all. It's hard to get my head around it sometimes—"

Robin shut him up by shaking her head. He looked crestfallen for a second, then propped up his crooked grin, trying to put on the brave front.

"'No,' huh?"

Robin smiled. "Let's say 'maybe.' But there's a lot to overcome before it's possible."

"I know. We've got all this history—"

"That's not what I meant."

He raised his eyebrows in question.

"You need to grow up, Sam."

He looked surprised. "I'm older than you."

"But you're not a serious person. You're a trickster, like that coyote I brought you."

"I thought you liked joking around."

"Need I remind you that, a few minutes ago, I was inside Ernesto's trunk? No idea if I would live to see morning?"

He winced. "This thing's gotten out of hand."

"It's not just this, Sam. It's all of it. The boosts and the chop shops and the cops snooping around. I don't want to keep living that way."

He wedged his hands into his pockets and stared at his shoes.

"Look," she said, "I know it's fun. And it's lucrative. Mitch put me through college with hot cars. But it can't go on forever. I don't want to get caught. I don't want to do time."

He looked up at her, and his wide mouth was pressed into a thin line. "You want to go legit. That Internet business."

"Yes, I do. And I don't want to start a romance with a criminal."

Sam pulled his shoulders up and glanced at Way-Way. Robin shivered against the cold, waiting.

"I don't know, Robin. Hard for me to imagine going straight. I'm thirty-seven years old, and I've never held a job in my life."

"Maybe you could come in with me. Work at the shop."

Their eyes met, and it seemed like a long time before he answered.

"I'd rather be your boyfriend."

That made her laugh. Sam grinned. She said, "Everything comes with conditions."

"Ain't that the truth. Seems like a lot to ask. Change my whole lifestyle just so we can go out on a date."

"Might be worth it."

"It might at that. Let me think about it. First I need to get us out of this mess."

"Can't you just let it go?"

"I'd be glad to, but Ortiz doesn't see it that way. And the cops are all over me."

"Count me out," she said. "I've had enough of guns and gangsters."

"I don't blame you. But maybe, when it's over, we can take up this conversation again."

He looked a little desperate, and Robin softened. She leaned toward him and kissed his smooth cheek. "Call me when it's over."

43

SAM HADN'T EXPECTED to sleep much, but the painkillers took care of that. When he awoke, bright sunlight oozed around the curtains. Someone was banging on his door.

He fumbled into his bathrobe and went to answer it with a pistol in his hand. As soon as he saw Stanton and Delgado waiting outside, he ditched the gun and opened the door.

"You guys working early today?"

"It's eleven o'clock," Stanton said. "Even you don't need that much beauty sleep."

Stanton pushed his way into the room. Delgado, smiling, followed him.

"Why don't you fellas come on in?" Sam said. "I'll make some coffee."

"Don't bother," Stanton said. "I've had plenty."

"I didn't mean for you," Sam said. "I'm full of Percocet. I need some caffeine to clear the cobwebs."

They followed him to his tiny kitchen, and watched while he started the coffeemaker.

"Up late?" Stanton asked.

Sam shook his head, but didn't volunteer any information.

"We know where you were last night," the lieutenant prodded.

"That right?"

"Weren't you at Morelos Automotive, down on South Broadway?"

"Nope. I had dinner at The Tropics, then came home, and went to bed. I've recently been under medical care, remember?"

Stanton's florid face brightened. He puckered his lips, looked like he wanted to spit.

"You didn't go see Ernesto Morelos?"

"Ernesto? Gosh, I haven't seen him in ages. How's he doing?'

Delgado snickered, but he stopped when his boss shot him a look.

"Not so good," Stanton said. "Someone locked him in the trunk of his car last night. He was there for hours before some deputies found him and let him out."

"No bathroom in there," Delgado said. "Ernesto's got a bad case of diaper rash."

Sam tsked and poured himself some coffee. He offered cups to the two cops, but they declined. The coffee was hot as hell, but Sam poured it down his throat anyway. He needed the jolt.

"Who put him in the trunk?" he asked.

"He won't say," Stanton snarled. "But my money's on you."

"I don't know anything about it."

"Ernesto's nephew is in the hospital," the lieutenant added. "Someone shot him and he nearly bled to death. Two of his friends were badly hurt, too. One of them's still unconscious."

"That's fascinating. But why are you here, telling me about it?"

"Because you did it, asshole," Stanton said. "I know you did."

Sam tried to act surprised, but the cops weren't buying. He glanced over at Delgado, who looked amused as hell.

"You really enjoy your job, don't you, Sergeant?" Sam said.

"It's the best," Delgado said. "You want to learn about humans, being a cop is better than being a sociologist."

"What have you learned lately?"

Delgado pointed a finger at Sam, sighted along it like it was a gun. "You, for instance, think you're a joker. You're so busy being cute, you don't even know when you're in deep trouble."

"How am I in trouble?"

Stanton stomped off into the living room. Sam passed close to Delgado as he followed, and the detective murmured, "Better watch out. He's pissed."

Once they were all in the living room, Stanton wheeled and said into Sam's face: "I *know* it was you who dumped Ortiz's stolen cars at Ernesto's place. Way I got it figured, Ernesto tried to get even last night and you and your friends one-upped him. Put his boys in the hospital and locked Ernesto in the trunk of his own car."

Sam smiled. "You got any evidence?"

"That you were there?"

"That I have any friends."

Stanton's blue eyes bulged. A vein pulsed in his forehead, looked like it was ready to pop. Delgado stepped between them, facing Sam, and gave him a shushing look.

"Can you prove your whereabouts last night?" the sergeant asked.

"I was at The Tropics, like I said. Ask anybody over there. Probably a dozen people who could vouch for me."

"How late were you there?"

"I wasn't wearing my watch."

"Then you came home and went to bed?"

"Just like any other good citizen."

Stanton muttered a curse, then pushed Delgado out of the way. He pointed a gnarly finger at Sam's nose.

"Listen, you. I *know* you were at Ernesto's last night. It's out of our jurisdiction, but the sheriff's department is pursuing every lead, and we're helping. We've got the bullet that hit the nephew, and we're running ballistics test. We're taking fingerprints. If you so much as exhaled in that place, we'll know it."

"I didn't say I've *never* been there," Sam said calmly. "You probably could turn up a fingerprint or something. But it doesn't prove anything. Ernesto's not talking?"

"That bastard will talk eventually. I'll offer him a sweet deal, drop the charges that are pending against him, if it means I can get you."

Sam didn't like the sound of that. He had no doubt that Ernesto would roll over for the cops.

"Go do what you have to do," he said. "But until you've got some proof, maybe you could stop dropping by at the crack of dawn every other day. That qualifies as harassment. I'd hate to file a complaint with the police commission."

It didn't seem possible that Stanton's face could get any redder, but a flush rose up his neck and onto his cheeks. Made Sam think of overheated mercury in a thermometer.

"You son of a—"

Delgado snagged his boss' sleeve. "Hold up, Lieutenant. We're not getting anywhere."

"That's right, we're not." Stanton glared at Sam. "Not yet. But we'll be back. And soon."

Stanton stalked out the door. Delgado shook his head at the lieutenant's behavior, then turned to Sam.

"The DEA's interested in you," he said. "That's the only reason we're not hauling you in right now and handing you over to the sheriff. But the lieutenant won't wait forever."

Sam shrugged, and Delgado headed for the door.

"Hey, Sergeant," Sam called after him, and Delgado turned around. "Stay away from Robin Mitchell."

A grin flickered on Delgado's face. "Why?"

"She's spoken for."

Delgado's eyebrows bounced, but he was still grinning. Then he left, pulling the door closed behind him.

44

SAM LISTENED TO A LOT OF MUZAK before Agent Rhetta Jones finally came on the line at the local office of the DEA.

"Mr. Hill. Glad you called. Your twenty-four hours are nearly up."

"I thought you were going to keep APD off me. Stanton was just here, threatening to bust me. Said some guys got shot up last night and he wants to blame me for it."

A pause, then Jones said, "Did you do it?"

"Of course not. I've been minding my manners. But how am I supposed to help you when I've got APD breathing down my neck?"

"There's only so much we can do with the local law enforcement—"

"Do you want my help or not?"

"Of course, but you didn't seem interes—"

"I don't like it, no. Makes me feel like a rat, calling you at all. But I need to get on with my life *without* Stanton all over me. Going along with you seems to be the only way to do that."

"We can help," Jones said quickly. "I'll call Lieutenant Stanton and tell him—"

"I don't care how you do it. Just take care of it. That asshole shows up here again and you'll never get Phil Ortiz. At least, not with any help from me."

Jones said nothing for a moment. Sam pictured her on the other end of the line. Her prim suit and her horn-rimmed glasses and her lips pursed over her prominent teeth.

"So," she said, "do you have some information for me? About Ortiz?"

"Yeah, I've got something. Remember you said he had a shipment coming in? I hear it's tonight."

"How good is this infor—"

"I'm still checking it out. I'll call you as soon as I have something solid. But have your people ready to move."

Again, a pause. Sam wondered idly whether she was taping the conversation.

"We can be ready," she said. "But I need some details."

"I said I'm working on it."

"Don't get excited. I'm sure you're doing your best."

"Just get Stanton off my tail."

"I'll take care of it," Jones said. "I'll get my boss involved."

"Whatever. I'll call as soon as I've got more on Ortiz."

Sam started to hang up, but Jones said, "Mr. Hill?"

"Yeah?"

"This wouldn't be another one of your little tricks, would it?"

"Tricks?"

"If we find out you're playing with us, my partner's not going to be happy."

"Tell your partner it's for real. And get him ready for tonight."

45

PHIL ORTIZ WAS ENJOYING HIS LUNCH when the telephone rang.
A salmon steak with a sprig of dill, roasted new potatoes, fresh
asparagus. Phil fancied himself a gourmet chef, and did nearly all
his own cooking. Best way to make sure the food was prepared
exactly the way he wanted it.

He believed in eating well, in treating each meal as if it were his
last. One never knew when death might come—particularly in his
line of work—and what could be more regrettable than ending
one's life with a belly full of fast food?

Phil applied this philosophy to everything in life. He enjoyed cars,
so why shouldn't he have every one his heart desired? He enjoyed a
comfortable home, so why not build one that was safe and warm and
perfect in every detail? Sophistication and comfort required money,
and he'd do whatever it took to keep himself rich and happy. If it
required breaking laws and committing sins, Phil would deal with
that in the next life. For now, he'd enjoy this life as much as possible.

The ringing telephone distracted him from his meal. Normally
he'd let one of his men answer it, but they were out in the garage,
cleaning up after Sam Hill and his gang of thieves, trying to get the
burnt rubber off the concrete floor.

Phil sighed and pushed back from the table. He leaned over to an
antique sideboard where a phone rested and lifted the receiver.

"Hi there, Phil. Know who this is?"

"I was just thinking about you," Phil said.

"I'm flattered."

"Don't be. I was thinking about your death."

"Uh-uh-uh, Phil. Not on this phone. You're tapped, remember?
Call me back on a safe phone."

Hill rattled off a number and hung up. Phil went into the next room, got a throwaway cell phone from a drawer. Untraceable.

When Hill answered, Phil said, "You interrupted my lunch."

"Tough. You want to eat or you want to hear what I have to say?"

"Depends on what it is."

"How about this—I've got your Impala. And I want to give it back."

Phil's face warmed. "You already used that car as bait once. What trick you got planned this time?"

"No tricks. I just want this all to be over."

"You should've thought about that before you boosted my cars."

"You should've given more thought to having your boys work me over. I steal cars, Phil, it's what I do. You fucked with me when you've got a whole garage full of expensive cars. You should've known better."

"I want those cars back. All of them."

"Forget it. Your collection's gone for good. Except for those Ernesto ended up with. You can get those back from the cops."

"Morelos is looking at a long stretch in prison." Phil didn't care about Morelos. His mind was whirring, trying to figure a way to rope Sam Hill into rounding up the lost cars.

"That one's your fault," Hill said. "You sicced Ernesto on me. I can't help it if he's too stupid to stay out of trouble."

"He's an idiot," Phil agreed.

"Then why mess with him? Let's cut out the middleman. This is a one-time offer, Phil. One low-rider with Our Lady of Guadalupe painted on the hood. You get your car back and I go on with my life."

"Why give it back?"

"I don't need it anymore. I'm done with you. You want it or not?"

Phil thought about the stash of heroin under the Impala's hood. He'd made a grave error, using the car as a drop point. But his buyer had been right there in Santa Fe, and it had seemed so simple. The heroin would only be hidden there overnight. Private security guards all around. What could've been safer? Until Sam Hill gummed up the works.

"I want it," Phil said. "That car's the only reason you're still walking around."

"How about tonight?"

"What's wrong with right now? Bring the car to me here."

"No way. I don't want to be anywhere around you or your boys. I hand over the car, and you might make me disappear."

Exactly what Phil had in mind. But there would be time for that later. First, make sure the car—and the heroin—were recovered intact.

"All right. We'll do it your way. Where and when?"

"I'll call you at nine," Hill said. "Tell you where to pick it up."

"And where will you be?"

"Nowhere you can find me. I'm leaving town. The cops are driving me crazy. I can't work in Albuquerque anymore."

"What if I don't like this idea?"

"Then I take the car to the mesa and torch it."

"No, don't do that. I want that car back."

"And I want to keep breathing. I give you the car, and we call it even. Got it?"

Phil thinking: No, we won't be even, you stupid bastard. Not until you're nothing but a pestering memory, decomposing somewhere. But he agreed. He told Hill the cell phone number, then began to warn him: No tricks this time …

But the car thief had hung up.

46

SAM SMILED, HAPPY WITH HIS PLAN. He had phone calls to make and arrangements to finalize, but first he needed to nail down a place for the transaction.

He pocketed his pistol, stepped outside, and locked up his condo. Looked around the verdant garden, making sure Ortiz's men weren't anywhere around, then strolled to the manager's unit. Joe Winter answered the door. Sam could hear Joe's wife at the far end of the house, sounded like she was talking on the phone.

"Speak to you a minute, Joe?"

"Sure, Sam. Come on in."

"Come outside. This is private."

Sam looked past Joe's head, toward where his wife's voice still chattered. Joe got the message and slipped outside, pulled the door closed quietly.

"What's up?"

"I think I've got a way to get out of this situation that's been bothering me."

"The cops and all?"

"Yeah. But I need to set up a meet for tonight. With a guy who's not so nice. Know what I mean?"

Joe's jaw jutted, and his pale eyes sparked. "I know the type."

"What I need is a place to put a car, where this guy can pick it up, but he can't find me doing it. Get the picture?"

"Parking lot at the airport, something like that."

"I was thinking of something enclosed."

Joe waited for it.

"Like an automatic car wash."

"One of mine?"

"They're just big enough for one car, and there's all that machinery in the way, so nobody races in at the last second and screws up the meet."

"I don't know, Sam. That's delicate machinery in there. It gets damaged—"

"Nothing will happen to it," Sam said. "I just want to slow things down. I put the car in there, the guy comes to reclaim it, he can't get the car out until I'm long gone. He drives away, then I come back a few minutes later, lock the place up again."

Joe looked at his feet and stuck out his lower lip.

"Sounds like a plan," he said finally. "Guy can't come chasing after you if his tires are hooked into the car wash. But if he tried, he might damage the equipment."

"Any damage, I'll pay for it. And it's worth a grand to me to use the place for an hour or so."

Joe's head snapped up. "No need for that, Sam. I told you, if you need any help, come to me."

"Still, you should be compensated. For the risk."

"Any chance the cops will trace anything back to me?"

"None."

"Then keep your money. I'll go get the keys."

"Thanks."

Joe turned to go back inside and Sam said, "Hey, Joe? This needs to be kind of isolated, you know? Not one of those that sits next to an all-night service station."

Joe flashed his oversized dentures.

"Already thought of that, Sam."

47

ALL THE ARRANGEMENTS were set by Thursday evening, but Sam made one more call before he went to meet Way-Way and Billy at the storage garage where Our Lady of Guadalupe was enshrined. Robin answered on the first ring.

"Hi there," he said.

"Sam. I didn't expect to hear from you. Thought you'd be out causing more trouble."

"Things are coming to a head. I wanted to talk to you before we—"

"Don't say it. I don't want to know."

That tripped him up. It was difficult enough, saying what he had to say, without her taking the hard line with him. When he couldn't spit it out fast enough, she sighed and said, "Why are you calling, Sam?"

"I've been thinking a lot about what you said. About us, I mean. Whether there can be an 'us.' And I want to say I'm willing to give it a try."

No response. He wished she'd say *something*, so he'd know whether to continue. Whether he was making a complete ass of himself.

"I, um, I'd be willing to try going straight and all that," he said.

Silence.

"I don't want to work at the shop," he said. "But I was hoping maybe you'd give Billy a job. He counts on me for his income, you know, and I thought I'd get him to go back to school—"

"That's all fine," she cut in. "But what are you going to do?"

"I don't know yet. I've got some money put away. I'll be all right for a while. Guess I'll find some kind of a job."

"You'd do that, just so you and I—"

"We could try it," he said quickly. "Like you said, it might be worth it."

"Think so?" She was teasing him now. He could hear the smile in her voice.

"If that's what it takes," he said. "I'd get out of the business. I'm getting too old for this nonsense anyway."

"Won't you miss the excitement?"

"Maybe I'll find another source of excitement," he said. "You, for instance."

"If we're going straight, I'll probably be pretty boring."

"I can't imagine that."

Sam waited. If she said no, he'd feel like a fool.

"All right," she said finally. "If you're serious about it, we can give it a try. But what about Ortiz?"

"I'm almost done with him. It should be finished tonight."

"Is that why you called now? In case something goes wrong?"

"I wanted you to know my, um, intentions. If my plan doesn't work, who knows where I'll be tomorrow?"

"Why don't you skip it? Let the cops worry about Ortiz."

"This is something I have to do myself. But then I'm through."

She let him hang on the line a long time. Had he said too much? Would she change her mind?

"Can I help?" she asked finally, and Sam felt another wave of relief.

"I want you to stay far away from all of this," he said. "I've already put you in danger once, and I couldn't stand to do it again."

"But—"

"No. I appreciate the offer, but I can't ask you to get involved, not if we're going legit. It wouldn't be seemly."

She laughed, but it didn't last long. When she spoke again, her voice sounded deadly serious.

"Be careful, Sam. I'd like to see how this dating business turns out. And I can't do it without you."

"I will. I'll call you tomorrow, after it's over."

"Then what?"

"I keep thinking about Vegas," he said. "Remember? You told me I ought to get out of town, take a vacation? Maybe I'll go, if you'll come with me."

"That's a pretty big step for a first date."

"We could take chaperones," he said. "Way-Way and Billy. Once this is done, we'll all need to get out of town a while."

"You make it sound so romantic," she said dryly. "A vacation with three fugitives."

"If this works out the way I think, we won't be fugitives."

"Don't say anything else," she said. "I'll be up all night worrying. Good luck, Sam."

48

WAY-WAY AND BILLY already were at the storage unit on North Fourth when Sam arrived. The overhead door was open, and Billy squatted behind the low-rider parked inside, illuminated by a flashlight that Way-Way held. The big man blocked much of the view, but it was pretty obvious Billy was changing the license plate on the car. Sam was glad no one was around to see it.

The only vehicles in the asphalt lot were Billy's Mustang and Way-Way's old van, parked side-by-side not far from Sam's rental unit. On the phone, he'd told them to wait until he got there, but he was glad now that they'd gotten started. It meant he'd spend less time out in the aching cold.

Sam killed his headlights, but left the engine running. He creaked out of the car. He still was stiff all over, but he hadn't taken even a Tylenol. He needed to be alert, and the pain would help. Besides, it served as a reminder of why he was taking chances, playing games with Phil Ortiz.

"Hi guys. Everything ready?"

Billy stood up from his post behind the low-rider. He had a screwdriver in his hand. "All set," he said.

Way-Way shut off the flashlight, and darkness settled over them like a black fog. They said nothing for a minute while their eyes adjusted.

"You two clear on what you're supposed to do?" Sam asked.

"I wanted to check one thing." Billy said. "After you call Ortiz, shouldn't I go to the car wash?"

"No. Give us the heads-up, then go to The Tropics and wait for us. We'll meet you there. I'll buy the drinks."

Billy said nothing more, just turned and slumped off in the darkness to his Mustang. The engine fired up a minute later and the car roared away.

"He's pissed," Way-Way said.

"I know, but it's better this way. If things go wrong, we could end up in jail. Billy wouldn't last long behind bars."

"But it's okay if *I* go to the pen for you."

"You'd be running the place within a week."

"Damned straight."

"Prison's probably the least of our problems," Sam said. "I imagine Ortiz and his boys will come armed to the teeth. I brought you a gun."

Sam dug a semi-automatic out of his pocket and handed it over. It looked like a toy in Way-Way's hand.

"Think I'm gonna need it?"

"Be better if we did this without a lot of noise. But take it just in case."

Way-Way stuffed the gun in his hip pocket and said, "You sure you want to let Ortiz drive this car away?"

"That's the plan."

"Then why wait there at all? Why not just dump the car and watch from a distance?"

"If we make it too easy, Ortiz will be suspicious. Besides, it'll be more fun this way."

Sam went into the garage, got behind the wheel of the low-rider, and sparked the ignition wires. He paused a second, appreciating the engine's throbbing baritone, then backed it out of the garage and swung it around to face the street.

Way-Way drove Sam's Caprice into the garage in its place, and locked the roll-down door. Then he trotted to his van. As soon as the van's headlights came on, Sam steered the low-rider south onto Fourth Street.

After the cold night air, it felt stuffy inside the car. Sam wore gloves and his leather jacket and two layers of shirts. He rolled his window partway down and let the night air come inside.

He unzipped his jacket and absently fingered the revolver stuck in the inside pocket. A bubble of anxiety worked its way through his guts. If everything went as planned, he and Way-Way should be completely safe. But things can always go wrong. Part of the plan depended on Ortiz doing what he'd said he would, and Sam knew better than to trust that.

49

JOE WINTER'S SPARKL-KLEEN CAR WASH sat back from North Fourth Street, just a few blocks from the 7-Eleven where Sam had first discovered Antonio Armas' corpse in the Thunderbird. Joe hadn't known that when he gave him the keys, of course, but Sam appreciated the symmetry.

The car wash was a windowless concrete shoebox with large overhead doors on each end and a solid, man-sized door set into one side. A couple of barrel-shaped, industrial-strength vacuum cleaners stood out front, and a dumpster was wedged into a corner at the back of the lot. Chain-link fences surrounded the car wash, separating the lot from a used car dealership on one side and a taco stand on the other. Both were buttoned up tight for the night.

Sam had used such car washes before. Customers pulled in off the street and drove around back, fed money into a device that looked like a robot, which stood sentry behind the building. They'd inch their cars forward until a chain-driven pulley system set into the floor caught the front tires. Slip the car into neutral, and the chain pulled the car through the car wash, a few inches at a time. Soapy water sprayed on the car, then big cloth brushes gave it a good beating all around, knocking off the dirt. As the car inched forward, another set of sprayers rinsed off the soap. Finally, four-foot-wide blowers air-dried the whole vehicle. Ba-da-bing, the car's clean and ready to roll again.

A streetlight at Fourth illuminated the front of the lot and another, over the dumpster, lit up the back. Enough light for Sam and Way-Way to see what they were doing but still some shadowy spots that would do for concealment.

Sam drove the low-rider around to the back of the car wash and left it there while he used Joe's key to unlock the side door. It was black as pitch inside, but he used a flashlight and found the wall switches Joe had told him about.

He hit one of the switches and the back door rolled up smoothly, letting in a little light from outside. Sam shined his flashlight around, let the beam track the drains in the floor, the big blue brushes hanging limply from the ceiling and along the walls, the gleaming sheet-metal vents of the dryers. Not many places to hide, but he'd need to be inside for what he had in mind.

Outside the open door, the low-rider sat waiting, Our Lady of Guadalupe staring up at the night sky.

"Okay, Virgin Lady," Sam said. "Feel like a bath?"

He got back behind the wheel and let the low-rider creep forward until it bumped over the second tow wedge on the ground-level pulley. Sam got out to check that it was all the way inside the building. The car was past the soap sprayers but still in line with the rinsers. Perfect.

"Sam?" Way-Way's voice came from the open door.

Sam stepped out from behind the brushes that hung vertically next to the wall.

"All set," he said. "Where'd you park the van?"

"Other side of that taco place. Nobody'll notice it over there."

Sam joined Way-Way outside. The car wash screened them from view of the street. Sam checked his watch under his flashlight, then used his cell phone to call Billy.

"Everything in place?" he asked when Billy came on the line.

"Yeah. The phone's right where you said to leave it."

"And where are you?"

"Parked across the street, out of sight, just like you said."

"Good. I'm calling Ortiz now. Sit tight."

Sam turned off the phone and said to Way-Way, "What do you think? Over behind the dumpster?"

"I knew you'd say that. The one stinky spot on the whole lot, and that's where I get to hide."

"You got a better idea?"

Way-Way looked around the empty lot. "The dumpster it is. How long do you think I'll be stuck back there?"

"Just until Ortiz drives away. If he comes alone, then I won't even need you. You're insurance."

Way-Way's teeth glinted in the dim light. "But you don't expect him to come alone."

"We're about to find out."

Sam took a deep breath to steady his nerves. He dialed his phone.

50

PHIL ORTIZ PACED in his living room, waiting on the call. He didn't enjoy pacing, didn't like the way it made him look anxious, but he couldn't help himself. Johnny Murdoch, still as a statue on the sofa, didn't seem to notice. Phil wondered sometimes what went on behind Murdoch's dead eyes, but he always figured the answer was: Nothing much. Too many blows to the head over the years.

Phil peeked between curtains to check the yard. Albert and Deuce and another of his men, Julio, stood guard out there, in case Sam Hill tried something funny here at the house.

He let the drape fall closed, and paced the room again. He had his Beretta stuffed into his belt at the small of his back. He was ready, if only the goddamn phone would ring.

Sam Hill was late. Nine o'clock had passed a couple of minutes earlier, and Phil could barely contain himself. If this was another prank, Hill's idea of a joke …

Then the cell phone rang.

"Hiya, Phil," Hill said. "Ready to roll?"

"I've been ready. You said nine o'clock."

"Don't be in such a hurry. You'll get your car."

"Where is it?"

"Not so fast. I want to make sure you show up alone."

Phil's teeth clenched so hard, his jaw ached.

"First, go to the E-Z Food Mart over on Isleta. You know the place? Not too far from your house."

"I know it. It's closed this time of night."

"That's right. But there's a newspaper box out front. Pay your fifty cents like you're buying a paper. In the box, underneath the papers, you'll find a cell phone."

"What the hell—"

"Uh-uh, Phil. Do as you're told, if you want to see that Impala again. I'll call you there, tell you where to go next."

The phone clicked to dial tone.

"Damn it!"

Phil turned to Murdoch, who sat perfectly still, awaiting instructions.

"He's playing games," Phil said. "I've got to go over to the E-Z Mart and pick up a phone so he can call me again."

Murdoch blinked once. "What do you want us to do?"

"Julio stays here to guard the house. You and Deuce and Albert follow me in your truck, but hang well back, so nobody sees you. Watch to see I get the call. Then follow me. I don't know where he'll send me, but I want all of you there."

"Right, boss. Then what?"

"Then we'll pick up the Impala. If Hill's around, we'll nail his ass, too, but the main thing is to get home with that car. We can always kill that bastard later."

Murdoch let a little disappointment show on his face, but it vanished quickly.

"I'll tell the boys to saddle up," he said.

51

SAM NEARLY JUMPED out of his skin when his phone trilled five minutes later. He'd been expecting the call, but his nerves still got the better of him. Way-Way chuckled, and Sam shot him a look.

"Billy?"

"Yeah. He's made the pick-up."

"He alone?"

"Nobody else in that Mercedes he drives. He's standing beside it now, looking around, probably trying to spot someone watching."

"All right, hang up and I'll call him. We don't want to keep him waiting."

"Hold it, Sam. An old truck just pulled into the parking lot at the far end of the store. Looks like that Chevy his goon drives."

"Ah, that's what we were expecting. Good job, Billy. I'll call Ortiz now. You sit tight until they're out of sight, then head for The Tropics."

"You sure, Sam? I could follow them."

"You've done your part. Way-Way and I will take it from here."

Sam thumbed off the phone.

"Ortiz bringing the whole crew?" Way-Way asked.

"Looks like it."

Sam dialed the number he'd memorized. Phil Ortiz answered on the first ring.

"Good work, Phil," Sam said brightly. "You follow instructions very well."

"Fuck you."

"Now, now. That's no way to talk. You're getting your car back. You should be a happy man."

"Just tell me where it is."

So Sam told him.

"You're coming alone, right, Phil?"

"Like you said," Ortiz said tightly. "I follow instructions very well."

"Not that it matters. I'll be gone by the time you get here."

"You'd better be."

"Come and get your car. But hang onto that phone. I might want to call you again."

"Don't bother. But that car better by God be there—"

Sam hung up on him.

52

PHIL ORTIZ SLOWED as he reached the car wash fifteen minutes later. The hell was the matter with Hill, setting up the drop this way? Idiot could've put the car anywhere and made a clean get-away, but no, he's got to be cute, park the low-rider in a fucking car wash. Was that supposed to mean something?

Phil let the Mercedes creep into the parking lot. Sure enough, his Impala was silhouetted inside the car wash. Big doors were open on both ends, and Phil could see through to the other side. He looked around for a trap, then drove to the back of the concrete-block building and cut the Mercedes' engine.

He sat in the car for a minute, scanning the parking lot. Still nobody. Phil had half-expected that Hill would have cops standing by—he already had a story ready if the police swarmed him. But there was no one.

He got out of the car, the Beretta in one hand, Hill's cell phone in the other. He tucked the phone into a pocket of his leather blazer as Murdoch's pickup bumped into the lot and drove right up to him. The three men were packed tight inside the cab, Murdoch behind the wheel.

"Everything okay?" Murdoch asked.

"Seems to be," Phil said. "Nobody around."

"Want me to drive the low-rider?"

"I'll do it. You watch my back. Deuce can drive the Mercedes back to the house."

Deuce smiled at the prospect of driving the boss' sleek car. He held a black Uzi in his lap. He shifted the mean-looking gun to his other hand, popped his door open, and got out. Albert scooted across to the passenger side, looked grateful to have more room.

Murdoch got out of the truck, pistol in hand, and followed Phil over to the dark car wash.

"Why'd he leave it in here?"

"Shit if I know," Phil said. "The guy's got a screw loose."

"Want me to go in first?"

"No, wait here. Just keep your eyes open."

Phil kept the pistol pointed straight ahead, near his hip, in case someone was hiding in the car. The low-rider looked okay, but, as he got closer, he saw the back window was riddled with cracks. Goddammit.

Phil peered through the windows, but the car was empty. He popped open the driver's side door and the dome light came on inside. The velvet upholstery was unblemished and the chrome-link steering wheel gleamed.

Then something moved, to his left, behind one of the big brushes that hung near the wall. He turned, bringing up the pistol just as he spotted a pale hand hit one of the red buttons on a control panel on the wall.

Freezing water battered Phil from all directions, blinding him, soaking him.

"Shit!" he screamed as he dived into the safety of the low-rider.

A shot cracked loudly inside the car wash.

53

As soon as Sam hit the button to start the water, he lunged out the side door of the car wash. A shot rang out, but he didn't think it came from Phil Ortiz. Probably Murdoch, standing back far enough to avoid the water, able to see inside.

Sam sprinted toward the rear of the car wash. The Mercedes and the pickup truck were back there, and Sam raised his own pistol, ready to fire if Murdoch stuck his head around the corner.

The big Indian bailed out of the truck, crouching as soon as his feet touched pavement. Looked like he held a jack handle. Sam could've shot him as he dodged behind the building, but he held up. Let Way-Way deal with that guy quietly. Sam wanted Murdoch.

He got his wish. Murdoch whirled around the corner and his big revolver spat fire at Sam.

One bullet whistled past his ear, but Sam didn't know where the other one went. He was too busy diving through the air, hitting the asphalt and rolling. Pain battered him from all sides, but he managed to end up on his stomach, facing toward Murdoch. He got off a couple of rounds, and Murdoch ducked behind the building. Sam saw that his bullets had punched two holes in Murdoch's pickup.

No cover on this side of the building, no place to hide. Sam needed to move. He clambered to his feet, his teeth set against the throbbing in his ribs and the hot pain of a skinned knee. He stumbled forward, toward Murdoch.

He heard an engine race and the shriek of Joe Winter's car wash equipment being violated, followed by the screech of wet tires. Ortiz, getting away. Sam glanced over his shoulder just in time to see the glistening low-rider bounce out into the street, its bumper throwing sparks.

Someone screamed behind the car wash and Sam nearly smiled. Way-Way.

Murdoch peeked around the corner of the building and Sam fired at him, chipping a chunk out of the concrete as Murdoch ducked back again. Damn, Sam thought, I told Joe I wouldn't damage the place.

He pressed against the wall of the car wash, his gun held up near his face, waiting for Murdoch to reappear. He was halfway between the side door and the corner of the building and was taken by surprise when the door crashed open behind him and Murdoch came flying out in a cloud of steam. The ex-boxer was soaked and he tried to blink the water from his eyes, but he still had the pistol in his hand.

Sam whirled and fired, saw blood erupt from Murdoch's meaty shoulder. The impact turned him halfway around. The gun went flying from his hand and clattered across the pavement.

Murdoch caught himself and squared up, facing Sam. He shook out the wounded arm and put up his dukes. Rocked his head, loosening up his thick neck. His narrow eyes dared Sam to use fists rather than bullets.

"Fuck that," Sam said, and he shot him in the thigh.

The bullet knocked Murdoch's leg out from under him, and he hit the ground hard.

Sam closed on him as Murdoch got his hands under himself, trying to push upright. Sam kicked him in the ribs, flipping him over.

The boxer raised up on an elbow, still trying to get to his feet. Sam kicked him on the chin, and Murdoch fell backward. Two more kicks to the head, and Murdoch didn't move anymore.

Sam turned, ready to rush to the back of the car wash and help Way-Way, only to find the big man standing before him, his beefy arms crossed over his chest, an Uzi dangling from one hand. Way-Way was smiling, and he wasn't even breathing hard.

"You okay?" he asked.

"Yeah," Sam said. "He never laid a glove on me."

Way-Way grinned. "That was good work. Kicking a man when he's down."

"Fool tried to treat this like a fistfight." Sam looked at the fallen man. "Too bad he blacked out. I wasn't done."

"That the guy who beat you up before?"

"Yeah."

"Hell, kick him some more, if it'll make you feel better."

"No time. Cops'll be here any second."

Sam ducked through the side door of the car wash and hit the buttons to turn the machinery off and close the doors. Then he was back outside, limping along after Way-Way.

"What is that? An Uzi?"

Way-Way held up the gun, looked it over. "Think so. Never seen one before."

"Where did you get it?"

"Took it off one of these guys back here. He never got off a shot."

As he spoke, they rounded the corner of the car wash. Phil's tattooed goon lay face-down on the blood-spattered pavement. The Indian was flat on his back, out cold. As they passed the downed men, Way-Way said, "That sumbitch tried to hit me with a tire iron." He sounded offended.

"You kill 'em?"

"Nah. Did you want me to?"

"Maybe next time."

The chain-link fence was six feet high. Way-Way grabbed Sam's leather jacket and boosted him over, then scrambled over behind him. They trotted around the back of the taco shack to the van.

As Way-Way climbed behind the wheel, he said, "Ortiz got away in the low-rider?"

"Yeah," Sam said. "Headed south. I'm guessing he's going home."

"So what happens now?"

Sam pulled himself into the passenger seat, grinning through the pain.

"I've got one more phone call to make."

54

PHIL ORTIZ SHIVERED with cold as he steered into his driveway, but he was happy to have the Our Lady car in his possession again, and he couldn't wait to put it back in the garage. More importantly, he wanted to check under the hood, make sure the goods were where they belonged.

He'd outfoxed Sam Hill this time. Phil glanced at his Rolex, wondering whether Hill was dead yet. No way he could've escaped. Not with all three of Phil's men there. He just hoped Murdoch and the others got away before the cops showed up.

He looked around his property, but he didn't see any sign of Julio, the man he'd left to guard the house. Probably in the kitchen, Phil thought, drinking my beer.

He fished a remote control out of his jacket pocket as he came to a stop outside the brick garage. Lights were on inside, and Phil could see the nearly empty room through the windows. Soon, he'd fill the garage with cars again, parked in neat rows, ready for car shows and prizes and the future glory of Phil Ortiz.

He hit a button to turn off the alarm, then another to make the door roll up. Phil waited until the door had finished moving before he let Our Lady creep into the building. When the car was in the very center of the garage, he cut the engine and opened the door and climbed out. He brushed at the damp spot his wet clothes had left on the upholstery, then let his eyes run over the car's green skin, checking for damage. He found a dent on the front bumper, but nothing that couldn't be easily fixed. The car wash had even rinsed away the dust.

Phil raised the hood. Everything seemed intact. He turned the wing nut on the fake air filter and lifted the lid. The package inside made him smile.

He caught movement out of the corner of his eye. He leaned around the open hood to see out the garage door, thinking maybe it was Julio, but the doorway filled with men with guns. Some wore SWAT helmets and black Kevlar vests and they pointed assault rifles his way. Others wore navy-blue windbreakers, the letters "DEA" glowing in white.

Phil froze. His pistol was in the glove compartment, where he'd stashed it after retrieving the car. Not that he would've tried to shoot his way out anyway, not with all those rifles pointed at him.

"Hands up!" one of the agents shouted. He was a big, raw-boned man in a windbreaker. Brock. A black woman with buck teeth stood beside him, her feet spread, a Glock pointed squarely at Phil's sternum. She looked serious as hell.

Phil put his hands up.

"Step away from the car!"

He did as he was told, though the car was the only comfort in the room now. He glanced back at the open hood, at Our Lady of Guadalupe, the Blessed Virgin. How could she let this happen to him?

Then hands were all over his wet clothes as the agents patted him down. They roughly pulled his arms behind his back and cuffed his wrists.

Phil finally found his voice. "What the hell is this?"

"Federal agents," Brock said. "Don't move."

"You have a warrant? You come busting in here—"

"Shut up." This from the little black woman with the glasses. Something about her poise made Phil obey.

The SWAT team spread out, checking the garage, but of course finding no one else. Then Brock stepped around to the front of the low-rider.

"What are you doing?" Phil cried. "Stay away from that car."

Brock shot Phil a look that shut him up. He disappeared behind the hood of the car, then reappeared a moment later, the package in his hand.

"Got it," Brock said.

"The fuck is that?" Phil said.

"Like you don't know," Brock said. "I'm guessing it's heroin. Lab tests will tell us soon enough."

"That's not mine. I don't even know how it got there."

The black woman started reading him his rights. Phil was so stunned, he could barely register her words.

Then realization hit. Sam Hill had set him up. One more joke at Phil's expense.

Phil knew he'd had the last laugh. Hill must be dead by now. That's the only thing that would make all this hassle worthwhile.

The agents roughly grabbed him by the elbows and hustled him out of the garage. Phil glanced back over his shoulder, got one last look at his beautiful low-rider, then he was shoved into the feds' plain, ugly car for the ride to jail.

55

SAM AWAKENED TO KNOCKING on Friday. He put on his bath-robe, then unplugged the clock radio beside his bed and carried it with him to the door, the power cord dragging along behind him.

He opened the door to find agents Brock and Jones outside, as expected.

"Morning." He held up the radio. "Could either of you use an alarm clock?"

The agents glanced at each other, frowning.

"Seems I don't need it anymore," Sam said. "Every morning, I wake up to cops banging on my door."

Brock's eyes narrowed. "Funny. Mind if we come in?"

"I'll make coffee."

They followed him into the living room, and stopped there while he went on into the kitchen.

"Do we have to go through the whole coffee-and-hospitality routine?" Brock asked.

"It's not for you. I need caffeine if I've got to face you two first thing in the morning."

He told the agents to make themselves at home, and they took their usual positions on the sofa, waiting. When Sam finally had a cup of strong brew in his hands, he joined them, sitting in the armchair.

"You seen the news?" Jones asked.

"Nope."

"We arrested Phil Ortiz last night. Found him in possession of four kilos of black tar heroin."

Sam smiled. "Is that right? Good for you."

"The heroin was found in the engine compartment of Mr. Ortiz's car," Jones said. "Just as you'd told us it would be."

Sam said nothing, waiting for it.

Glowering, Brock said, "So the question becomes: How did you know the heroin would be in that car?"

"It's like I told Agent Jones yesterday," Sam said. "I heard it on the grapevine."

"See, here's what I don't understand." Brock continued as if Sam hadn't said anything. "We've been after Ortiz for years, and he's never—and I mean *never*—anywhere near the drugs he moves. He uses two, three layers of people to mule the stuff. Loyal people. No way we could trace it back to him. So what's he suddenly doing in a car with heroin under the hood?"

"Sounds like he made a mistake."

"Worse yet," Jones said, "he'd reported the car stolen weeks ago, from a car show up in Santa Fe. You know anything about that?"

Sam shook his head.

"That makes the case against him weak," she said. "If the car was out of his possession for weeks, his lawyers could argue that somebody else put the drugs in there."

"Sounds to me," Sam said, "like Ortiz faked the theft. Maybe you could charge him with insurance fraud, too."

The agents exchanged a look. It wasn't a happy one.

"There's another thing," Brock said. "APD located Ortiz's Mercedes in the parking lot of a car wash up on North Fourth. They'd gone there after getting reports of shots fired. Three guys were there, and somebody had beaten them up and shot one of them a couple of times. They're all in the hospital."

"Really?"

"That's right, and Ortiz was soaking wet when we arrested him," Jones said. "I suppose you don't know anything about that, either?"

"Not me. Who are these guys?"

"They work for Ortiz. All have criminal records."

"Then why do you care how they got hurt? More criminals out of circulation, that's a good thing, right?"

Brock stood up, looked like he wanted to slap Sam silly.

"No, it's not good," the agent said through gritted teeth. "It's more unanswered questions. Ortiz's lawyers could have a field day with that."

"What does Ortiz say? He know anything about why those guys were in his Mercedes? Were they getting his car washed?"

"He's not talking," Jones said, and Brock shot her a look. "Hasn't said a word since we busted him."

"Relying on his lawyers, huh? Boy, that sure sounds like 'guilty' to me."

"We don't care how it seems to you," Brock said. "We only care what a jury thinks. If Ortiz walks because you've pulled some shenanigans with this stolen car—"

"'Shenanigans?' That doesn't sound like me. I'm a serious person, trying to stay out of trouble."

Sam leaned back in the armchair. He was enjoying himself.

"You called Ortiz's house yesterday," Brock said. "We've got you on tape."

"And?"

"What was that about?"

"Just trying to verify my tip," Sam said.

"You told him his phone was tapped, and to call you on a safe phone."

"He already knew it was tapped, so that didn't matter. I was just nailing things down. I wanted to make sure he'd be ready for you."

The agents didn't look pleased.

"So why are you here?" Sam asked. "My tip turned out to be good. That's all you wanted from me, right?"

"No, that's not all," Brock said. He remained standing, looking down at Sam. "We'll need you to testify. Tell the court how Ortiz had his thugs beat you up. Testify how you knew about that low-rider with the heroin in it."

Sam slowly shook his head. "You don't want that."

"Don't tell me what I want, goddammit."

"Quincy," Jones said, a caution in her voice. "You'd better sit down."

Brock ignored her.

"Look, you little smartass," he said to Sam. "This case has got more holes than a screen door. If we don't have you testifying for our side, you can bet your ass that Ortiz's lawyers will call you in and try to trip you up."

"I've got no interest in testifying."

"We could force the issue."

"You might not like what I say on the stand."

"We'll issue a subpoena—"

"If you can find me," Sam cut in. "I might be out of town for a while. I've been thinking about taking a vacation."

Brock's face flushed and he clamped his lips shut.

"Wait a minute," Jones said. "That might be for the best. If Ortiz's lawyers can't find him—"

"It's no good," Brock said sharply. "We need this guy on our side. If he disappears, it just raises more questions we can't answer."

Jones scooted forward on the sofa and adjusted her tweed skirt around her knees. She peered at Sam through her thick glasses.

"What about the witness protection program?" she said. "You agree to testify for our side, and we can get you into the program, set you up somewhere in a new life."

"No, thanks."

"Let me tell you something, buddy," Brock said. "You're gonna need some protection."

"Thought Ortiz was in jail."

"For now. But he has long arms."

Sam got to his feet and cinched tight the belt of his bathrobe. He gave the agents a smile.

"That's a chance I'll have to take," he said. "But, hey, I'm not too worried. You guys are the federal government. You won't let Ortiz loose."

"He'll send people after you," Brock said. "You'll be in danger the rest of your life."

"They won't find me. I'll be on vacation."

"You planning to make this 'vacation' last forever?"

"If need be," Sam said.

He moved toward the door, and the agents took their cue and followed. Brock looked like he was chewing on something. Maybe his own tongue.

"I tell you what," Sam said. "Let me give you a little parting gift."

"What?" Brock snarled. "Your alarm clock?"

"Better than that. A way to tie Ortiz to the murder of Antonio Armas."

That froze them in place.

"In exchange," he said, "I expect you to stick to your word and keep Lieutenant Stanton out of my life."

Jones nodded. Brock glared at Sam, waiting.

"Okay, then," Sam said. "When you arrested Ortiz, did he have a cell phone on him?"

Jones hesitated, then said, "Two of them."

"And you've got them now?"

"Bagged and tagged."

"Check 'em out. I think you'll find one of them used to belong to your informant."

Brock's eyes widened. "How would you know—"

"No more questions," Sam said. He opened the door. "Just go check it out."

The agents, surprise still registering on their faces, stumbled out the door and turned back to look at him.

"Thanks," Jones said and she smiled, forgetting for the moment about her buck teeth. "We'll do that."

"So long," Sam said.

As the door swung closed, he heard Jones say, "Have a nice vacation."

56

A WEEK LATER, Robin Mitchell came out the front door of the Mandalay Bay resort to find Sam, Way-Way, and Billy sitting on a bench beside the half-circle driveway, basking in the sunshine. The temperature was in the sixties—short-sleeve weather—and the sky was so bright, all three men wore sunglasses.

Robin smiled when she saw them. She'd been smiling a lot since she and Sam and the boys arrived in Las Vegas. More relaxed than she'd been in a year. Part of that was getting away from the stress of running the garage. The other part was Sam. He'd arranged everything: Four adjoining rooms upstairs (all registered to his fake ID), flowers, limo rides, romantic dinners every night. Sam, ever-resourceful, pulling strings and greasing palms and taking care of things, creating the best damned "date" any girl could hope for.

For her part, she'd managed to—mostly—not think about the situation back in Albuquerque. The cops still sniffing around. Phil Ortiz and his henchmen being arraigned on a long menu of charges. Her business running on inertia while she was gone.

It couldn't last forever. Eventually, she'd have to go home, with or without Sam. But they were having a lot of fun in the meantime.

"There you are!" she said as she approached the trio on the bench. "I've been looking all over for you."

"We couldn't stand it in the casino anymore," Sam said. "Too noisy."

"Yeah," Way-Way said. "And all those little old ladies keep staring at me. Gives me the creeps."

"What are you doing out here?" she asked.

"We found something else to bet on," Sam said. "Billy says he can name the make and model of every car that pulls up."

"How's he doing?"

"I think we owe him two hundred bucks so far," Sam said.

Billy beamed. "Gonna use it to pay my tuition to mechanics' school."

"You finish upstairs?" Sam asked her.

He'd left her there earlier, after a room-service breakfast together. Robin had been engrossed in the Internet, keeping tabs on business.

"I'm done for now," she said. "Sold a Chevy engine to a guy in Illinois."

"Good," Sam said. "We need the money."

Robin laughed. "What do you mean 'we,' cowboy?"

"Hey, I've got to make something," he said. "This vacation's costing me a fortune."

"Too bad you can't get it back from Phil Ortiz somehow," she said as the three of them made room for her to sit next to Sam.

"Hell, that guy ended up *costing* me money. I had to pay off Joe Winter for shooting up his car wash."

Robin made a shushing face and glanced around to make sure no one was listening.

"You might want to watch your mouth," she said.

"I'd rather watch yours."

She smiled, but got distracted as a red sports car growled into the driveway. All three men turned to watch.

"Ferrari F40," Billy said. "A 1988, I'm guessing. Looks like the one Tom Selleck drove on that TV show, *Magnum, P. I.*"

"Nice car," Sam said. "Wonder what something like that would bring on the resale market?"

"I could get forty grand for it, easy," Robin said automatically. Then she caught herself. "I mean, if we were still in that business."

As they watched, a sporty guy with an expensive haircut got out from behind the wheel and went over to talk to a parking valet. He left the car running and the driver's door open.

"Forty grand?" Sam said. "Hell, that'd pay for a vacation, wouldn't it?"

Robin said, "*Sam.*"

Way-Way and Billy were grinning.

"Come on, Robin," Sam said. "Look at this freaking guy. He left the engine running."

Robin rolled her eyes, but then she smiled and shrugged.

Sam got up off the bench and casually strolled toward the idling Ferrari.

"Be right back," he said.